T0162332

ONE MAN'S
TRASH

ivan e. coyote

ONE MAN'S TRASH

[stories]

Arsenal Pulp Press
VANCOUVER

ONE MAN'S TRASH
Copyright © 2002 by Ivan E. Coyote

2nd printing: 2012

All rights reserved. No part of this book may be reproduced or used in any form
by any means – graphic, electronic or mechanical – without the prior
written permission of the publisher, except by a reviewer, who may
use brief excerpts in a review, or in the case of photocopying,
a license from the Canadian Copyright Licensing Agency.

ARSENAL PULP PRESS
101, 211 East Georgia Street
Vancouver, B.C.
Canada V6A 1B6
arsenalpulp.com

The publisher gratefully acknowledges the support of the Canada Council
for the Arts and the British Columbia Arts Council for its publishing program,
and the Government of Canada (through the Canada Book Fund) and the
Government of British Columbia (through the Book Publishing Tax Credit
Program) for its publishing activities.

Book and cover design by Solo
Cover photograph by Rosalee Hiebert
Printed and bound in Canada

NATIONAL LIBRARY OF CANADA CATALOGUING IN PUBLICATION DATA:
Coyote, Ivan E. (Ivan Elizabeth), 1969-
One man's trash

ISBN 1-55152-120-2

I. Title.
PS8555.O99O53. 2002   C813'.6   C2002-910490-4
PR9199.3.C66825O53 2002

ISBN13 978-1-55152-120-6

This book is dedicated to Richard Spencer,
Luna Roth, and the one and only
Shelley Frankenstein,
for putting it to music.

I would like to acknowledge the support and
tireless work of Blaine Kyllo, Brian Lam, and
Robert Ballantyne at Arsenal Pulp Press,
for going above and beyond
so many times for me.

I would also like to thank the other editors I have
had the opportunity to learn from: John Burns
of the *Georgia Straight* for his keen eye and kind
heart, Teresa Goff at the now sadly defunct
loop magazine, Yvonne Gall at CBC Radio, and
Gareth Kirkby at *Xtra! West*.

I would also like to thank my guardian angel,
who insists on remaining anonymous.

"Mavis for Prime Minister" first appeared in *loop magazine*. "Weak Nine" first
appeared in CRANK magazine. An earlier version of "More Beautiful" first
appeared in the *Georgia Straight*. "Stupid Man," "Older Women," and "Fish
Stories" were originally Loose End columns that appeared in *Xtra! West*. "Fear of
Hoping in Las Vegas" was earlier published in *Xtra! West*, a multi-media version
was on CBC Radio's *120seconds.com*, and it also appeared on-line on *nerve.com*.

THEN

NOW

THERE

THEN

The Queen Mother

My grandmother, Florence Daws, born Florence Lawless, keeps a newspaper clipping carefully folded into a tin in the right drawer of the dining room bureau.

The box also contains old photographs, cards, birth and death certificates, her passport, the brass door knocker that family legend has it my grandfather – when he was a young guard during the war – stole off of Winston Churchill's back door, and assorted locks of hair and baby teeth.

But it is the newspaper clipping that begins this story. It was the front page of the *Yukon News*, dated February 19, 1969. It is a photo of my mother shaking hands with Jean Chretien, our Prime Minister.

Our Prime Minister now, of course, not then. Back then he was just a minister of something or other, probably not all that important or he wouldn't have been in the Jim Light Arena in Whitehorse, Yukon, at the Ice Capades shaking hands with a nineteen-year-old girl.

Not that my mother was just any girl. She wasn't yet my mother, of course, but a young maiden who had just been crowned Rendezvous Queen. She is smiling prettily at him, and her tiara is sparkling. Jean Chretien is not looking at her, but at the cameraman, smiling from only one side of his face, as he still does today.

Rendezvous is quite a big deal to Yukoners, even now.

Rendezvous is our winter festival, held each February since the Gold Rush, they say, to fend off cabin fever and give frostbitten and exhausted miners a chance to cut loose.

We have flour-packing and log-sawing contests, dog sled races, sourdough pancake breakfasts, a longest beard contest for the fellas, and a hairy leg contest for the ladies. It is winter in the Yukon, after all.

We have the Keystone Cops, who tow a cage on wheels behind a Studebaker and blow whistles and burst into pubs to arrest men without facial hair and ladies without garters. Then they drive you around town in the cage with their sirens on until you donate money to charity, and then drop you off at a different bar.

People get very drunk and play pool with toilet plungers.

And then, of course, there is the Rendezvous Queen.

Every business in town sponsors a candidate, who then must demonstrate her ties to the community, sell tickets that pay for prizes, perform a talent, and make a speech on what she would do if elected.

Potential Rendezvous Queens must also be female. And unmarried.

The winner gets a blue sash and a tiara, copious bouquets of flowers, and a trip around the world.

My mom also won a fur coat and a food processor.

Mere weeks after her victory (her queenly duties had thus far consisted only of shaking hands with Jean Chretien, announcing the skaters at the Ice Capades, cutting the ribbon on the new Robert Service wing of the museum, and selling tickets for the Shriner's lottery at the mall), my mother was tragically forced to step down as queen, which meant giving back her fur and appliances and turning over her tiara to her runner-up. Needless to say, she didn't get the trip around the world either.

She was pregnant, you see. Four months along and due in August, and thus engaged to my somewhat shell-shocked father, who was working in a bridge-building camp somewhere near Teslin Lake.

After a brief round of rumours, they were married in June. My dad poured the foundations for our house on Hemlock Street, bought a welder and a flatbed truck, and gave up his dreams of returning to

New Zealand to work on the swordfish boat.

My mom's nemesis, Brenda Fraser, stepped up and became Rendezvous Queen. She broke three toes on her trip around the world when she slipped getting out of a gondola in Venice. She returned to Whitehorse early and was married that summer and pregnant before the leaves fell.

Every once in a while, when me and my aunties and gran get to smoking cigarettes and drinking black tea and telling stories, we pull out the tin box and sort through the photos.

Every time we do I hear the story of how my mom was Rendezvous Queen once upon a time and then had to give back the crown and the fur and the trip, on account of how she was pregnant with me.

They tell me this like I am somehow guilty of stealing this honour from her, like it is somehow my fault that I came along and she was prematurely stripped of her tiara, and the beauty queen dream of every girl.

Every girl except me, of course.

I smile at how beautiful and radiant she looks in the newspaper clipping. How rosy-cheeked and long-lashed and glowing. How pregnant with me she looked.

Thirty years later, in 1999, someone decided that for this year's festivities they were going to do a Rendezvous Queen retrospective. They were going to contact as many previous queens as they could, throw them a dinner, and take their pictures wearing their sashes and altered versions of their royal dresses.

My mom was contacted by a Rendezvous volunteer, someone who was not a Sourdough as we say, as in, not a real Yukoner, also referred to as someone from outside. She was sent an invitation, got her hair done, and bought a new dress. She had made her own gown back in '69, but she had stopped sewing years ago.

A couple of days before the dinner she got a phone call from Brenda Fraser, her runner-up and fur inheritor. Brenda informed my mother that there had been a mistake, that the volunteer had been from out of town. That the volunteer had gotten my mom's name off of an old list. That the volunteer couldn't possibly have known what of course my mom and Brenda knew too well, which was that my mom had only been queen for a couple of hand-shakes and an Ice Capades and had been forced to step down because Rendezvous Queens were supposed to be single young maidens and my mother had found herself in the family way.

My mom and dad had been split up more than two years, and my mom had transformed herself from a recent divorcée who was concerned about who would mow the lawn into a still beautiful bachelorette who could light her own pilot light and operate a power drill with confidence and finesse.

"What a crock of shit," she told Brenda firmly, but politely. "We are approaching a brand new millennium here, and you are not going to tell me I can't go to the reunion because I got pregnant thirty years ago. It is archaic and small-minded to suggest it. Besides, I won fair and square. As far as I'm concerned, you owe me one fur coat and a food processor, sweetheart."

My mother went over the head of Brenda the beauty queen and talked to the Rendezvous board of directors. They were sheepish and apologetic, and insisted that of course she could come. She was, after all, the reigning Rendezvous Queen of 1969 and besides, hadn't she gone on to make quite a success of herself, and by the way, how is your daughter?

Time has a way of getting revenge, especially on beauty queens. I saw the pictures. My mom wore a pale blue dress, with a simple corsage, and looked every inch a royal lady.

Brenda Fraser, on the other hand, was frumpy and puffy in her pale green number, with the blue sash stretched across her middle like the string on a ham.

My mother looks serene, and thoughtful. Her face is a little more tan than the rest of the Rendezvous Queens, probably from cross-country skiing with her friend Rhona up the street.

My mother looks at least ten years younger than the woman standing next to her does, the now divorced real estate agent who was crowned in 1976.

It Doesn't Hurt

My cousin claims he invented the game, but I swear it was me. You need what they call a rat-tail comb, one of those plastic ones you can buy at the drug store; they come in bags of ten. They have a comb part, and then a skinny plastic handle, which, I suppose, is where the name comes from.

You take the comb and heat it up over an element on the stove so you can bend a curve into it, like a hockey stick. Then you get a ping pong ball, or one of those plastic golf balls with the holes, and there you are. Comb ball, we called it. Let the game begin.

The game was invented to be played in a long, narrow hallway, so a mobile home is the perfect stadium. You close all the bathroom and bedroom doors, and each opponent gets on their knees at either end of the hall. Kind of like a soccer goalie, only shorter. Whoever has the ball goes first.

You hold the handle of the comb in one hand and bend the comb back with the other, and let go.

The ping pong ball rebounds off the walls and floor at speeds approaching the sound barrier, and the other guy tries to block the ball with any part of his completely unprotected body.

A ping pong ball striking naked skin at the speed of sound is bound to hurt. So there were the obvious injuries: circular welts about the face, neck, and arms were common. There were other hazards, too: carpet burn, bruised elbows and knees. Once, my sister leapt up to block a shot and smashed her head on a door handle and just about bit the tip of her tongue off. My cousin sprained his wrist trying to flip himself back onto his feet for a rebound.

My aunt stepped in, in an attempt to reduce the casualties. She tried to ban comb ball altogether, but was met with such a united front of dismay and pouting that she was forced to compromise. We were only allowed to play until someone cried. And we had to scrub off all the little white marks the ping pong balls left on the wood panelling.

We were only allowed to play until someone cried. Of course, this added a masochistic element to the game we all enjoyed. I would take a stinging shot to the lower lip and kneel motionless in the hallway, breathing deep through clenched teeth. Everyone would stop, searching my face for any sign of moisture, which would signal the end of the game. "Doesn't hurt," I would whisper bravely. "It doesn't hurt. It doesn't hurt. Let's go. My shot." Everyone would let out their breath and continue.

Whoever cried ended the game. Whoever cried sucked. My aunt would march in and grab our combs, and send us outside to play. "It's a beautiful day out there. Quit killing each other in my hallway and go get some exercise."

Playing outside was okay, but there was nothing like a rousing, bloody match of comb ball. We would compare scars afterwards, like soldiers. "Took the skin right off, bled all over the rug too," we would brag, our striped shirts pulled up over our elbows. "And not one tear. Kept right on going."

My cousin Christopher ended it all the day he broke his thumb. This required a trip to emergency, and a splint. He forgot to try not to cry, and the combs were confiscated for good. For a while we were impressed with his sling, and his need for painkillers, but then reality set in. No more comb ball. Christopher was a wimp, and prone to accidents. Remember, he got that concussion that one time and they took the tire swing away? We all mourned the loss of the greatest game that ever came to the trailer park.

We came up with a version of cops and robbers that satisfied our bloodlust for a while. It involved riding around on our bikes and wailing on each other with broken-off car antennas, but it wasn't the same. Crying while playing outside was a different story, because you got to go back into the house. The stakes weren't as high. There was nothing to lose. I worry today, about my friends' kids. Nothing hurts when you play Nintendo, not even when you die. What are we teaching our children? I still utilize the skills I learned playing comb ball. Just the other day, I fell off the back of a five-ton truck helping my friend move. I leapt up immediately, exclaiming, "It doesn't hurt. It doesn't hurt." And a couple of weeks later, it didn't. Just like the good old days.

My Hero

Webster's New School and Office Dictionary defines a hero as a man of distinguished courage, moral or physical; or the chief character in a play, novel, or poem.

Her name was Cathy Bulahouski, and she was, among other things, my Uncle John's girlfriend. She had other titles, too – my family is fond of nicknames and in-jokes – she was also referred to as the girl with the large glands, and later, when she left John and he had to pay her for half of the house they had built together, she became and was remembered by the men as "lump sum." The women just smiled, and always called her Cathy.

Cathy Bulahouski, the Polish cowgirl from Calgary. I've wanted to tell this story for years, but never have, because I couldn't think of a better name for a Polish cowgirl from Calgary than Cathy Bulahouski.

I remember sitting in her and John's half-built kitchen, the smell of sawdust all around us, watching her brush her hair. Her hair was light brown and not quite straight, and she usually wore it in a tight braid that hung like a whip between her shoulder blades. When she shook the braid out at night, her hair cascaded in shining ripples right down her back to just past the dips behind her knees.

She would get John to brush it out for her, she sitting at one end of a plain wooden table, he standing behind her on their unpainted plywood floor. I would be mesmerized, watching her stretch her head back and showing the tendons in her neck. Brushing hair seemed like a girl-type activity to me, but John would stroke her hair first with the brush, then smooth it with his other hand, like a pro. My father rarely touched my mother in front of me, and I couldn't take my eyes off of this commonplace intimacy passing between them.

The summer I turned eleven, Cathy was working as a short-order cook at a lodge next to some hot springs. She was also the horse lady. She hired me to help her run a little trail ride operation for the tourists. My duties included feeding, brushing, and saddling up the eight or so horses we had. And the shoveling of shit. I wasn't paid any cash money, but

I got to eat for free in the diner, and I got to ride Little Chief, half Appaloosa and half Shetland pony, silver grey with a spotted ass. Cathy and I were co-workers and conspirators. Every time we got an obnoxious American guy she would wink at me over his shoulder while he drawled on about his riding days in Texas or Montana, and I would saddle up Steamboat for him, a giant jet black stallion who was famous both for his frightening bursts of uncontrollable galloping and for trying to rub his rider off by scraping his sides up against the spindly lodge-pole pines the trails were lined with.

I always rode behind my aunt; Little Chief was trained to follow hers. Her horse would plod along at tourist speed in front of me, and I would try to make my legs copy the way hers moved, the seamless satin groove her hips fell into with every swing of the horse's step.

Sometimes we would ride alone and she would whistle and kick the insides of her boots in and race ahead of me. Little Chief would pick up the pace a bit like the foot soldier he was, and my heart would begin to pound. Cathy would ride for a while and then whirl her horse around, her long braid swinging around and hanging down her front as she rode back towards me.

One day we were lazily loping alongside the little road that led back to the hot springs when one of

Cathy's admirers came up from behind in a pick-up. He honked hello as he and his road-dust drove by, which spooked Little Chief and he bucked me off.

On impact, tears and snot and all the air in my lungs were expelled. I lay on the hard packed dirt and dry grass for a minute, bawling when I could catch little pieces of my breath.

"Get on," Cathy said, hard-lipped as she rode up beside me. "Get back up on that horse right now. Do it now or you'll be too afraid later."

She was tough like that.

One Christmas Eve shortly after she and John had finished drywalling, our family all had turkey dinner out at their place. We were each allowed to open one present, and my mom had suggested I bring the one shaped just like a brand new toboggan from under our tree at home.

The coolest thing about Cathy was how she would gear up in a snowsuit in thirty below in the blue black sky of a Yukon night (which begins at about two in the afternoon around solstice) and go play outside with the rest of the kids. Not in a grown-up, sit-on-the-porch-and-smoke-cigarettes-and-watch kind of way, but in a dirty-kneed, get-roadrash-kid kind of a way. Right after I ripped the last of the wrapping paper off my gleaming red sled, she was searching through the sea of snowboots by the door for her black Sorels and pulling her jacket off the hook behind the door.

"Let's go up the hill behind the house and give it a try. Not much of a trail in winter, but we'll make one."

I suited up right behind her, followed by my sister and a stream of cousins with mittens on strings.

It was so cold outside that the air burned arrows into the backs of our throats and frost collected on our eyelashes above where our scarves ended, which would melt if you closed your eyes for too long and freeze on our cheeks.

We packed as many of us onto the sled as we could so everyone could have a go. We rode and climbed, rode and climbed until our toes began to burn. "Once more, everybody goes one more time, then we should go in," Cathy breathed through her scarf. She pushed her butt to the very back of the sled, and motioned for my little sister to shove in front of her, between her legs. I jumped in the front, and my little sister's snowsuit whistled up against mine as she wrapped her legs around me. The toboggan's most alluring feature was the two metal emergency brakes on either side, with the black plastic handles molded to fit the shape of your hand. I tried to grab both and steer, but my sister also wanted to hold onto one, and started to whine. "You can

each have one," Cathy ordered. "You steer one way
and you can steer on the other side, okay you guys,
don't fight about it, everyone else is waiting for their
turn. Let's go."

About halfway down we flew off a bump. My
little sister hauled on her brake and we screeched off
the path and smashed into a tree. Cathy's leg hit first
and I heard a snap.

By the time we rolled her onto the sled and
pulled her back to the house, her face was glowing
blue white and her teeth were chattering. John
came running out with a flashlight. He gingerly
pulled up the leg of her snow pants, and dropped it
again, his face changing from Christmas rum red to
moonlight white.

"Jesus Christ. Get the kids in the house and pull
the truck around. And get her a blanket, she's going
to emergency. Pat, are you okay to drive?"

A weird silence took over the house after they
left. I fell asleep in my clothes on the spare bed and
barely woke up when my dad carried me out to the
truck hours later.

"Did Cathy live?" I whispered into his ear. He
smelled like scotch and shampoo and his new sweater.

"She's fine. She's asleep. She's got a cast and a
bottle of painkillers. You can call her in the morning."

I told my friend Valerie all about it the next day,
bragging like it was me. "I tried to save us, but my

sister is too little to steer. Cathy's bone was poking right out of her leg, and she never cried once. There was even blood. Now she has a little rubber thing on the bottom of her cast so she can walk a bit, plus she has crutches."

"My dad cut the tip of his finger off with a saw once. They sewed it back on," she reminded me.

"Yeah, but you weren't even born yet. Besides, a leg is way bigger than a finger. Hurts more."

Later that winter the wolves got hungry because the government sold too many moose hunting licenses, and dogs and cats started to disappear. Cathy phoned me one Sunday morning and told me that they had found what was left of Little Chief at the bottom of the mountain the day before.

"I didn't tell you yesterday because your mom told me you had a hockey game. I know you're sad, but horses and wolves are animals, and they follow different rules than we do. He had a good horse life, and now the wolves will make it until spring. You were too big to ride him any more anyway, and your little heart will get better in time. Wolves are wolves and men are just people."

She was tough like that.

When she left John, she was tough too. She took her horse and one duffle bag, and most of his savings to cover her half of the house. She never even cried. Or that's how I saw her leaving in my mind. Dry-eyed in her pick-up, with the radio on and a cloud of dirt-road dust from the Yukon straight back to Alberta.

Bet she never looked back, I thought.

My uncle started to date one of the other cooks from the lodge. She had a university degree so everyone called her the professor.

My little sister grew up and moved to Calgary. She, like myself, inherited our family loyalty, and looked Cathy up.

My mom and I went to visit my sister at Christmas, and she told me Cathy would love it if I could make it out to visit her in Bragg Creek. But we got snowed in, so I called her the day before we left.

Cathy's voice sounded the same as I remembered, except more tired. "I can't believe you're almost thirty years old. I remember you as just a little girl with that white hair and filthy hands, little chicken legs. You had such big eyes. My God, you were cute. Just let me grab my smokes."

I could hear dogs barking and a man cursing at them to shut the hell up. A television droned in the background.

She sounded out of breath when she got back on the phone. "Here I am. Hard dragging myself around since my accident. Did Carrie tell you about my legs?"

MY HERO

She had broken both of her femurs straight
through a couple of years ago, and had pins in her
knees. She still had to walk on two canes and
couldn't work any more.

"I lost the trailer," she explained. "Couldn't get
worker's comp because it happened on a weekend,
and the unemployment ran out a year ago. Had to
move in with Edward and lie about being common
law even to get welfare."

"What are you saying about me?" I heard the
man's voice again in the background. "Who you
talking to anyway?"

"My niece. Turn down the TV for chrissakes."

"You don't have any nieces. You don't even have
any brothers or sisters."

I presumed this was Edward. He obviously
didn't understand family loyalty the way we did.
Blood and marriage were only part of it.

"'Member that time you broke your ankle on
the sled? You didn't even cry. You were my hero
back then, you know?"

"Well, I cried when I broke my legs this time.
I'm still crying. Some fucking hero I am now, huh?"

I heard the empty in her voice and didn't know
what to say. So I told her a story.

"Your old shed is still out behind John's, you
know. Nobody ever goes in there. A couple of years
ago John said I should go out and see if your leather

33

tools were still out there. Might as well, since maybe I would use them, and so I did. It was like a time machine in there. Everything was still hanging where you left it.

"I took down your old bullwhip. It didn't really want to uncurl, but I played with it a little and it warmed up a bit. I took it outside into the corral and screwed around with it. On about the hundredth try or so, I got it to crack. I got so excited by how it jumps in your hand when you get the roll of the arm right that I hauled off and really let one rip. The end of the whip came whistling past my head, and just the tip of it clipped the back of my ear on the way by, and it dropped me right into the dirt. I was afraid to peel my hand from the side of my head to see if there was still an ear there. Hurt like fuck.

"But I thought of you and made myself try a bunch more times until I got it to crack again, you know, so I wouldn't be too afraid next time. Like you would have done."

She was quiet for a while on the other end of the line. "You still have some imagination, kid. Always did. You gotta come visit me sometime. I'd love to see what you look like all grown up. I don't get into Calgary much any more, only when Edward feels like driving, which is never. You'd have to come out here. Carrie could give you directions."

I've been back to Southern Alberta twice since

then, but never made it to Bragg Creek to see Cathy Bulahouski, the Polish cowgirl from Calgary. She can't ride any more, she told me, and I couldn't bear to ask her if she had cut off her hair.

Just Reward

She was never that good at Frisbee, but it wasn't about that for me. Her summer brown legs bent with a grace I could never possess, and her straight black hair swung unbraided, always a strand or two across her face, in her mouth.

Her palms were lighter than the backs of her hands, and often she would lay them in the place her hips would be one day, plant both feet in the dust, and throw her head back when she laughed.

She was doing just this the day we found the money. Her Frisbee throws were unpredictable and wobbly, and this one had arced sideways into the juniper bushes that lined the parking lot next to the parched park we were playing in.

Nothing is as dry as July dust in the land of the midnight sun, so I almost missed the brown leather wallet laying in the dirt.

"Valerie, come look here. Look at this."

"I don't want to look at bugs. Come on, throw it here."

She saw the look on my face and went silent, looked down into my hands.

A rectangle of worn calfskin with a brass bill clip inside, pinning down a wad of American bills. I stuffed it into the waistband of my shorts and we ran down to the edge of the river, under the cover of willows.

Eleven one hundred dollar bills, two twenties, four ones.

"One thousand, one hundred and forty-four dollars." Valerie was perched on the balls of her feet, her teeth shining white behind chapped lips. "We have to take it to the police station," she whispered.

"The police? Are you crazy? We could buy practically anything with this."

She shook her head, a wrinkle creasing her forehead. "Our parents would take it away anyhow. The police." She said this like there was no other option.

"We could hide it for a while then, in the fort. We could save for our educations." I appealed to her practical side.

"If we take it to the police, and they can't find whose money it is, then we can keep it. We could be heroes." She raised her eyebrows and rubbed her palms on her shorts for emphasis. "Rich heroes."

It was settled then. I never once thought to argue that it was I who had found the money. I had no name for what I felt for her; we were nine years old and I would have done anything she wanted.

"You fucking did what?" My father was chewing his pork chop with his mouth open.

My mom slapped his arm, right above where his shirtsleeve was rolled up to. "You did the right thing. I'm really proud of you girls, and so is Valerie's mom."

My father looked at me like he couldn't figure out just where he had gone wrong.

The policeman shook his head as he filled out the form. "Well, he was probably an American." This guy was sure to make detective. "No ID, huh?" He narrowed his eyes at us, beads of sweat on his forehead.

We shook our heads simultaneously.

"Beginning of summer, probably on his way up north. To Alaska," he explained, as though there was a multitude of destinations for tourists to choose from. "There's a chance he'll check in on his way back down. No one claims this in six weeks, say, then you two are in the money."

We spent that money over and over in our heads for the rest of the summer. Valerie wanted a camera, and an easel and paint set. "No cheap stuff. The kind of brushes with horse hair in them."

I wanted a BMX with chrome pedals, and a

microscope. "Maybe a chemistry set, too. And walk-ie talkies. One for me, one for you. We could talk on them late at night. And a rowboat."

"Cowboy boots," she added, swinging in the hammock, a piece of straw between her front teeth. "Red cowboy boots."

It was the ninth of August. We had seven days left.

The next morning, the phone rang at exactly eight o'clock. I was eating puffed wheat and listening to "Seasons in the Sun" on the radio that sat between the toaster and the plant on the lemon yellow counter next to the window. My mom was filling the kettle, and held the phone between ear and shoulder, motioning silently at me to turn the music down.

"She's right here. I see. Okay, I'll tell her. Thank you, officer." She uncurled the phone cord with her forefinger and hung it up. "Someone claimed the wallet. He's downtown, he wants to give you two a reward. I'll drop you both off on my way to work."

We sat side by each in the back seat of my mom's Tercel, silent and lead-bellied under our seat belts. Valerie smelled like Irish Spring soap and toothpaste. I had forgotten to even brush my hair.

He looked like a caricature of a tourist come magically to life. The buttons of his polyester print shirt strained to hold his belly inside his khaki shorts. He even had waxy hairs sticking out of his ears. He shook our hands, his moist palms unnaturally soft. "Here's my little heroes," he wheezed. He patted us both on our heads, mussing our hair and smiling at the cop behind the counter. "Let's head across the street and get you girls your *re*-ward."

He stood perspiring in the service window of the Dairy Queen. "What's your favourite flavour of milk-shake?"

"She likes strawberry, chocolate for me," I piped up. Talking to strangers was my job. Explaining why we had done what we did to parents was her territo-ry, but strangers were my area of expertise.

"Too early for milkshakes," she whispered to me, as he pulled out his billfold and handed over the four singles. I shushed her. Surely this was just the first phase of our reward.

But ten minutes later we sat alone at the bus stop, the change from our milkshakes stuck to my palm, for bus fare. He had told us what good girls we were and hopped into his motor home. His wife had waved over her knitting at us from the passenger seat. The TravelEase edged back onto the road.

"I hate South Carolina. Never going there." Valerie spit in the dust and tied up her shoe.

My dad was still at home when we got back, strange at this time of day. He was smoking an

Export 'A', drinking tea, and reading *Shogun*. We tried to head straight into my room, but he looked up and cleared his throat.

"Whoawhoawhoa. Where're you two going?"

Valerie picked idly at a scratch on her thigh; I stood on one leg, then the other, waiting for the inevitable.

"Didja get your *re*-ward?" He split the word in two, like someone from South Carolina would.

I nodded almost without moving my head. Valerie shrugged.

"Welllll...?" His one eyebrow raised, his hands perched like spiders on the wooden table.

"We got milkshakes," Valerie said softly.

My dad turned his right ear to us, played with a make believe hearing aid.

"He bought us both milkshakes," I blurted out, the sweetness of chocolate already halfway back up my throat.

"Small or large?" he crowed, slamming both palms flat, slopping tea onto his paperback.

"Large ones." The bottom of Valerie's jaw stuck further out defiantly, her brown palms returning to her hips.

My dad laughed from deep in his belly at us both, and reached for his smokes. "Well, I hope it went down good, because that was the most expensive fuckin' milkshake you're ever gonna drink."

JUST REWARD

Twenty years later I realized we had, in fact, spent that money on our educations.

Three Strikes

I was about eleven when I moved into the closet.

It seemed perfect at the time – a cozy little shelf for a bed, situated close to the sock drawer, protected on all four sides. No hiding place for anything with furry hands to grab me. My closet had those accordion doors with the little wooden slats. You can see out of them quite well when you are up on the top shelf, making them excellent for reconnaissance purposes. I dragged a little reading lamp on an extension cord up to my humble fort and I was the king of all I surveyed.

My mother, who worried easily, was thoroughly disturbed, wondered if something was wrong at school. She never asked me outright, of course, just whispered questions to others when she thought I was out of earshot. "Do you think maybe someone tried something funny with her? Did any of your kids ever move into their closets?"

She had many reasons for her anti-closet-residing stance. I could electrocute myself up there with that cord. I was far less likely to ever make my bed. I could fall and break my neck. I could choke to death on my gum and no one would ever know.

Eventually, I gave in and slept on the ground in a bed like all the other mortals.

Years later, I recalled the episode. I couldn't help myself. "Just think, Mom, all that time you spent talking me out of the closet. You'd think you would be more pleased with how things turned out."

She found this neither witty nor ironic.

Gay Pride, 1990. Hand in hand with my organic food warehouse worker/political theorist girlfriend, I spot my mother. She is standing outside a shoe shop on Denman Street, wondering what the parade is about. Her eyes meet mine at the same time it dawns on her what everyone is all dressed up for. She spins on her heel and retreats into the store, pretending that she hasn't seen me.

I go for dinner with her that night, without the girlfriend. Neither of us mention what we did that day.

Christmas, 1999. "I have a funny story for you," my

mom whispers conspiratorially to me over the phone. "I think I ... how do you guys say it ... I think I 'outed' you today."

She was taking a knitting class. Her current project was a pair of wool socks for my girlfriend in Montreal. She had them almost finished, but forgot the stitch that finished off the top part. She called up her knitting instructor (who also used to teach highland dancing in her glory days) and asked her if she could pop by for a sock-closing-up stitch lesson.

"Come on by, dear, I know how worrying knitting can be, so close to the holidays."

My mom said she didn't even think about what she was saying. "So sorry to trouble you like this, but I really want to get these in the mail. They're for my daughter's girlfriend."

"You should have seen her face," my mom laughed. "A nice lady like myself, knitting socks for homosexuals. I'm so used to it all now, you know, and somewhere along the way I must have got over myself."

now

Clean and Sober

It all started with the jam jars. My mom was in town visiting, digging in my cupboards for mugs to pour us a cup of tea. She made that clicking sound of disapproval with her tongue and raised an eyebrow at me.

"You, my dear, are thirty-one years old. Don't you think it's time you stopped drinking out of jam jars?"

I jumped to my own domestic defense, pointing out that I actually had six jam jars that matched.

"See, Mom? It's a full set." I said this with feeling, as though Martha Stewart would be proud.

She shook her head. "We're taking you shopping."

We returned the next afternoon with a sparkling array of drinking receptacles. It turns out there are different glasses for water and highballs and even little ones for juice. Who knew? Even more surprising was that I acquired all sixteen for less than the cost of six jars of organic raspberry compote.

Doing dishes became an exercise in household pride. I liked to see my newest additions shining in my cupboard in neat little rows, like glass soldiers ready to jump forth and fight thirst. It inspired me to throw a dinner party. Vodka and cranberry, anyone?

I felt so grown up.

I got matching tea towels next, and four coffee mugs the same colour as my teapot. This move precipitated the purchase of an actual kettle, because grown-ups don't boil water in a soup pot. Everybody knows that.

I was unstoppable. I bought an almost brand new carpet from a set sale to replace the old worn rug in my front room.

One spring day I came home to find a scratch-and-win lottery ticket in my mailbox. It looked like a bingo card and claimed that if I was one of the lucky few to scratch the right boxes, I could be the proud winner of a set of steak knives, a framed picture of a mallard duck, or a brand new twenty-four-inch colour television. Steak knives? What luck! I'm not fond of beef, but I could use them to cut up other things. I answered the skill-testing question and called the number right away. All I had to do was let a nice salesman come 'round to my house and demonstrate a new product. Then I could claim my prize.

In less than an hour he was at my back door, a guy in his early twenties, perspiring from hauling a remarkably large box up my back steps. His shirt was wrinkled and he had those little tassels on his brown dress shoes.

"I didn't win the duck picture, did I? What I'm hoping for is steak knives." I explained this to him as he unpacked a rather complicated looking vacuum cleaner. It was sleek and black, with ergonomic handles. I wondered if he worried about scratching the paint. I would.

"Impressive machine you got there, young man." I cleared my throat. "What is one of these things worth, if you don't mind me asking?"

"Well, without the hepa filter, and drape cleaning attachments, or the steam cleaning unit, about sixteen hundred dollars. The whole package will run you about three grand," he said without looking up.

I almost dropped my matching mug.

"Well, being as I am recently unemployed, I should probably tell you right now that the chances of my spending the bulk of my retirement savings on a vacuum cleaner are fairly slim," I said politely. I felt I should be honest.

He stopped assembling and stood up with a sigh. He suddenly looked older. "Can I borrow your phone?"

He dialed the number from memory. "Let me speak to Charlene." He held the phone between his chin and shoulder, and looked at his watch. "Charlene, it's Ricky. I'm in East Vancouver. I'm still in East Vancouver, Charlene. Do you think you could find it in your heart to get me a client who has a job? Uh-huh." He scribbled something down, and hung up.

"Nothing personal, you know. Charlene gets paid by how many houses she sends me to, but I only get paid by how many units I sell."

I nodded in sympathy. He began to pack up his box.

"I guess this means you're not going to vacuum my floor for me then?" I was pushing my luck. He knew it, I knew it.

"You're lucky I'm letting you keep the steak knives."

"Hey, I won those fair and square. I bingoed and answered the skill te–"

"Everybody wins, lady. That's the deal. I haven't seen any colour TVs, though. Just a whole lot of steak knives."

"What about duck pictures?"

He shook his head, took his vacuum, and left me thinking on my back porch.

The world was indeed a treacherous place, and I needed a new vacuum cleaner. I share my attic apartment with two dogs, the evidence of which could be seen collecting in corners and on carpets. Tumbleweeds of fur appear daily under the bed, an uphill battle any pet owner can attest to, one that had been bothering me more and more since the jam jar incident.

My hand-me-down Hoover had expired in a gasp of smoke a couple of months earlier, and I had been borrowing my neighbour's ever since. It was a geriatric drag-along model which wheezed and complained whenever I plugged it in. Every Sunday I feared might be its last. It made a high-pitched whining sound when it rolled over area rugs, and I would almost feel guilty for making it work so hard. It had one broken wheel and should have been retired from active service. It had done its time and dog hair seemed a little too much to ask.

It was the first time I ever read a flyer, and it worked. I bought a new vacuum, just like the one in the ad. I was too excited to read the manual, much less watch the instructional video. A brand new re-conditioned Phantom ThunderVac with dual cyclonic action and on-board attachments stood shining triumphantly in my hallway. It even had headlights. I finally understood those guys who wax their cars by hand every Saturday.

I called my mother long distance. "Mom, guess what? I got a brand new vacuum. I am the proud owner of a remarkable advance in household cleaning. I am about to change the way I feel about carpets by harnessing one of nature's most powerful forces. As soon as I install my patented cleaning wand."

"Good for you, honey. Maybe my allergies won't act up so much when I visit at Christmas."

"It has a hepa filter, Mom. Are you allergic to hepas? Because they won't trouble you any more. Not in my home. . . . I'll call you back in a bit."

I hadn't felt this kind of anticipation since I was twenty-one and had a bag of magic mushrooms and a long weekend ahead of me. I plugged it in, and both dogs leapt onto the bed for safety. Poor things. They just weren't used to the sound of this kind of raw power in our living room.

"It only hurts the first time," I said to my cowering Pomeranian, and set to work.

Minutes later, I sat down and surveyed my spotless living room. My dogs sniffed around, as if unsure they were in the same house. "Go ahead, shed your little heart out," I told my husky. "I'm not afraid of you any more." I wished I had taken before and after pictures.

The phone rang. "Hi, Mom. It looks amazing in here. I can hardly wait for my house to get dirty again, and I have you to thank. This whole thing started with the jam jars."

"What are you talking about?" It was my friend Michelle. "Are you okay? You haven't been taking too much Nyquil again, have you?"

"Sorry. I thought you were my mom calling back." I knew Michelle wouldn't understand about the ThunderVac. She hadn't turned thirty yet and still boiled water for tea in a soup pot. She wasn't ready to relate to this kind of advanced home improvement.

"Whatever, man, I just wanted to see if you were into going for a beer."

I wasn't. What I really wanted to do was be at home, at one with my new vacuum cleaner. Besides, I couldn't afford a beer. I was saving up for cutlery.

Mavis for Prime Minister

I work in the movie industry, in the props department. This means it is often my job to hunt down and purchase strange and obscure items, which often takes me to strange and obscure places. This day was like any other, and I found myself somewhere deep in the suburbs, seeking cheap pieces of foam to stuff into luggage for a scene we were shooting the next day at the train station.

There is a certain kind of woman, we all have met one or two: they waitress in truck stops, balance budgets in banks, answer phones at car rental places, take your tickets in airports, and today, charge you for three hundred pounds of foam in a warehouse somewhere next to a river you don't know the name of but wouldn't fish out of. These women are all, of course, unique and special, but I have noticed certain character traits they have in common. They are somebody's grandmother, the evidence of which is usually thumbtacked close to where they work. They smoke at their desks. They wear cardigans, and still call a shirt a blouse and a pair of pants slacks. They are not the highest paid employees, but chaos ensues if they call in sick for work, which they very rarely do. When they take their yearly trip to Reno or Vegas, no one can find anything, and productivity grinds to a halt. They are the only ones who know how to fix the photocopier or where to find the keys for any number of places. At home, they never run out of toilet paper and outlive their husbands by decades.

This particular woman's name was Mavis and for me it was love at first sight. Her voice was like sandpaper taking candle wax off of an old oak table top, and she had me pegged right off the bat.

"You got a bed in the back of that piece of shit you call a van out there?" she asked, gesturing to the loading dock where two well-muscled lads were loading foam into my '72 Ford Clubwagon. "I thought as much. You need a piece of foam for it? Come with me, sweet pea, we'll fix you up."

She sold me a piece of four-inch-thick foam for twenty dollars, and instructed the boys to throw that in as well. She scoffed at me and shook her head when I told her I had been thinking of picking one up at Home Depot or something for a while now.

"What are you, made of money? You need foam, you come to me." That's another thing these women have in common. They always say things like "What am I, made of money?" or "I knew there was something funny about that guy right from the get-go," or "That's just how I am. Don't ask me to change."

I, for one, hope that she never does. The Mavises of the world keep things from falling apart.

As I started up my van, Mavis ground her cigarette out with the heel of her pump and winked at me. "There you go," she smiled, and nodded towards the back of my van. "Now she'll have something to rest her elbows on."

It was just as I suspected. Mavis doesn't miss a thing.

The Safe Way

It's almost impossible to look sexy in a Safeway, but she did. She had one of those long, lawless curls that fell into her eyes when she leaned over to smell the avocados, and she did that combination head-turn-blow-air-through-your-lips move to return it to its rightful place. That's when she met my eyes, and smiled.

I felt a flirt turn under my ribs. I smiled back, then pretended to compare prices of red russet versus golden nugget new potatoes. But when I looked up, she was gone, and standing where she had been was a man with thick fingers and wire brush eyebrows, bagging lemons.

I don't know if she purposely stood in the nine items or less line right behind me or not, but there she was. She had more than nine items in her basket, too. Maybe she was cruising me, or maybe she was a grocery rebel with no regard for her fellow shoppers, or maybe she just couldn't count.

I casually glanced into her basket, trying not to look like I was trying to look into her basket.

Two bricks of medium firm tofu, balsamic vinegar, alfalfa sprouts and assorted greens, four heads of garlic, chamomile tea, a bag of dried red lentil beans, and most tragic of all: Rice Dream, the dairy sustitute.

I felt her eyes pass over my chest, down my arms, and across my groceries.

I am about to purchase a block of cheese, eggs, a quart of milk, and one of those already cooked chickens. It's all over, I think.

But she passed a pink non-smoker tongue over her lips, shifted her weight with a smooth swing of velvet-clad hips, and winked at me.

She was flirting with me. What was she thinking? This couldn't work. She'd want to go on a hike or something, with plenty of fresh air punctuated by lectures on what I've still got in my colon or my lungs. I'd try valiantly to cook her dinner, but she'd be allergic to wheat, or my dog, or my hair pomade. She'd try to slip soy products in my coffee the next day, insisting that I'd never know the difference, but I always do.

I knew I couldn't keep up this charade any longer. She probably spelled woman with a "y." We were all wrong for each other.

But I was blushing. She had impossibly long eyelashes and her nipples were pushing at her t-shirt. And my eyes were caught in the hollow spot at the base of her neck and my lips wanted to touch her there.

I could wear my blue shirt and tie, and zip up her dress in the back while she stands in front of the mirror with a lipstick in her left hand, a colour called rubine or del rio or diva. I like expensive lipsticks; they're the only ones that don't make my neck break out in a rash.

She would turn smoothly towards me, raised up on her toes to meet my kiss. One cool hand would slip around to the back of my neck and she would hold my bottom lip in hers for just a little too long, and graze it with her teeth.

She would smell like essential oils, and soy milk, but I wouldn't notice. I would smell like expensive French deodorant and get dog hair on her velvet, but she wouldn't care.

Makeover

I liked it when she ran her fingers through my hair, even though she had ulterior motives. "How about just a blonde rinse, or maybe we could just frost the tips?" she would whisper into my ear, like foreplay.

She couldn't help herself. She was a professional. Hair was her thing. We had been dating for a couple of months and the reality was that I was not going to last unbleached or undyed much longer. I was sleeping with a colour technician, and my hair was, well, boring.

"It's not quite brown, but it's not really blonde either," she would wince, as though it pained her somehow. "Can't we just do . . . something? I could fix it."

"I didn't realize my hair was broken," I would retort, trying to lighten things up a little. But she was dead serious.

I caved a few days later, after two glasses of red wine. She wanted to bleach me blonde, but I was just about to turn thirty and I figured, it's now or never, buddy, both feet first. If you're gonna dye your hair, dye your hair.

"I want blue hair. The colour of a propane flame. Give me really blue hair. Quick, before I chicken out."

The thing that real girls never tell you is that it's true. They actually do have a higher pain tolerance than . . . well, the rest of us. Bleach hurts. But I got what I asked for.

Shining on top of my head was a crop of titanium-coloured fluff. It felt like August straw and my scalp hurt to touch.

I don't own much propane flame-coloured clothing, so dressing for work the next day brought on a deep and disturbing fashion crisis. I almost had to call in sick.

I didn't recognize myself. I would catch my reflection in windows out of the corner of my eye, and whirl around to find only me, in Technicolor, with clothes that didn't, that couldn't, match.

About a week later we were in the shower together when she let out a shriek that dropped a rock in my belly. "What do you think you're doing?" She looked panicked.

I looked down at the bar of soap in my hand. I was going to wash my hair.

"You can't use soap on colour-treated hair. You're killing me. You need a balanced alkaloid shampoo and a good conditioner. And you haven't been wearing your shower cap, have you? Do you think I don't know? You are impossible to work with. Your back is fading out already. Sit down in the tub. I'm going to have to touch you up."

"Look, if I had known it was going to be like this, I wouldn't have gone through with it," I sighed. "I liked how we were before. I didn't know it was gonna involve this kind of commitment. Maybe I'm just not ready for colour-treated hair. Maybe I just can't handle the responsibility."

She left me for a bisexual esthetician, and my hair faded to television screen blue, then for a couple of weeks I walked around looking like a seventeen-year-old boy who had prematurely greyed, then blond. A couple of hair-cuts later, I was back to nondescript, not quite brown.

Then I met the stiltwalker. Stiltwalkers possess a penchant for spectacle and costume. Stiltwalkers wear a lot of make-up. Everything was fine, until she spent the night.

I heard her scuffling around in my bathroom, going through my drawers. "You okay in there?" I asked her through the closed door.

"Where is your facial cleanser?" she called out.

"You're joking me, right? There's a bar of soap on the little shelf in the shower."

She shot out of the bathroom, looking disgusted. "I can't wash my face with a bar of soap," she said, incredulous.

Just what you can wash with soap is still a mystery to me. I must have missed that chapter in the handbook. Perhaps I was at hockey practice when they covered the proper uses of soap, not to mention the difference between pumps and open-toed mule shoes. I have a lot to learn.

"No make-up remover?"

I shook my head.

"Moisturizer?"

I shrugged, palms up.

"Okay." She shook her head. "Just tell me where you hide your hairbrush."

I was afraid to answer. My cupboards were bare. "I have mechanic's hand cleaner," I said hopefully. "It takes oil and grease off. It contains lanolin. It smells like oranges. . . ."

Turned out, if I were to properly entertain female company, I had some serious shopping to do.

The woman at Eaton's was very kind. I was overwhelmed, and slumped, my elbows resting on her cool glass counter.

"I thought you could wash your face with soap,"

MAKEOVER

I explained plaintively. "Can you help me?"

"Oh, honey, don't worry, I'll fix you up. I've worked with worse. You just need a skin profile. And a three-step regimen. It'll be okay. Repeat after me: cleanse, tone, moisturize."

Her eyes grazed over my shorn hair and flat chest, but she never blinked. She passed no judgment upon me for thinking toner was only for photocopiers, and I loved her for it. Her name was Madeline, and she spent forty-five patient minutes with me. Every time she leaned over to touch my skin I couldn't help but breathe deep in the smell of her. I had an almost unbearable urge to rest my head against her ample chest. I felt so grateful, I wanted to mow her lawn, or change her tires, or something.

Turns out I have combination skin, with a fair but clear complexion, most suited to spring colours. I spent seventy-two dollars, and left with a tiny bag of exquisitely packaged products.

Halfway down Granville Street, I recognized the swagger of one of my friends approaching, his hands deep in his pockets.

"Hey man. What'dja buy at Eaton's?" His voice was even deeper than last month, stubble starting to sprout on his chin and upper lip.

"You know, couple things," I almost whispered, trying to sound casual. "Rehydrating cream, stuff like that."

"Stuff like *what?*"

"It's rehydrating cream, okay? And a soothing cream cleanser. Oh, and eye supplement. I'm just holding it for a friend."

"Are you wearing mascara?" He narrowed his eyes at me, leaned over, and sniffed. "And each to their own and everything, buddy, but I gotta tell you, you smell kinda like . . . roses, man. You smell like flowers, dude."

I changed the subject. I didn't tell him I smelled of evening primrose oil, which uplifts and boosts your everyday moisturizer when applied beforehand. I didn't tell him that according to Madeline, you're never too young or too butch for a good three-step beauty regimen; five minutes in the morning, five at night. I didn't mention that I had just been exfoliated and that my face felt fucking great.

I didn't tell him that testosterone often brings on puberty-grade acne, and that he might want to invest in a good epidermal cleanser, perhaps even an astringent.

I didn't say anything. That is why they are referred to as beauty secrets. Because I, myself, plan to age gracefully.

The Test

When my union benefits finally kicked in, I decided to make good on my New Year's resolution: doctor, dentist, new glasses, the full tune-up. I take good care of my car, why not myself?

I like my doctor: late fifties, kind, doesn't balk at my tattoos or nipple rings, pretty much everything I need in a health care professional. I called and booked myself a physical.

A week Tuesday? Great. Her receptionist has a soft, sleepwalker-like voice. I can't imagine her in an emergency.

I didn't find out until I was in the waiting room that my doctor was on holiday, and that her replacement would be seeing me. I was vaguely disturbed, but sat down to wait. I was already there. I don't usually go to the doctor unless something is bleeding or about to fall off, and here I was being all responsible and stuff, no sense turning back now.

A young, fresh-faced dyke walked into the waiting area, glancing at the chart in her hand. She called my name. "Come with me," she said briskly. I followed her down the hall.

A new receptionist? How forward thinking of these guys to hire a queer receptionist. I like these community clinics. We sat down in my doctor's office. My chart was on the desk. Same posters on the wall: signs of domestic abuse, colour poster of male and female reproductive organs, wear your helmet or you could look like this watermelon here, nothing ominous to be found.

"So. . . ." the young dyke extended her hand. "I'm Doctor Giovanni. You're here for a complete physical?" I looked at her face. Not a wrinkle to be found. She looked fresh out of her wrapper. I thought medical school was supposed to be stressful.

Now, I don't mean to be ageist or anything, but I must admit there are instances where a person might naturally feel more comfortable with some-one of a more elderly persuasion at the helm: heli-copter pilot, flight instructor, bomb technician. And doctor. Doctor springs to mind.

I nodded. Try to act natural, I told myself. "So Doctor Witherspoon is . . ."

". . . on holiday. I'm filling in for her." She knit-ted her brow and searched my chart. "Don't I know you under a different name?" Her finger was resting on my legal name.

Know me? The cappuccino I just drank was now

also becoming disturbed. I was here for a pap smear, for chrissakes, she wasn't supposed to *know* me. This was a private affair, one to be conducted by a kind and ageing woman who lived in a big house far from this clinic. She had to shop and dine in places I did not frequent, and she did not know any of my friends, unless she had also examined their breasts for lumps in this clinic, in which case she would not know that they are my friends. . . .

"Ivan, right? That's you're other name. Thought I recognized you. You know, I could write it down here that you prefer to be called Ivan, they're pretty cool about that kind of thing here. I loved your book, by the way."

My doctor didn't know my other name because my doctor didn't need to. My doctor didn't read my books. Because my doctor did not have a brush cut like me, or baggy pants like me, and, oh, my God.

I looked at her again. I knew her from somewhere.

I could not get a pap test from anyone that I knew from somewhere. Especially when, in my panic, I could not place exactly where I knew her from. She was too young for us to have gone to high school together, thank Christ.

I kept my panic to myself. She must think me strange, I thought, this storyteller who hadn't said a word.

"So ... I'll give you a minute to undress and change into this" – she held up the prerequisite paper dress – "and I'll be right back. I'll go warm up my hands."

Was that a wink? Did she just wink at me? The door shut behind her and I quickly searched the room.

No windows. Okay, okay. Plan B. I tried to figure out how to call myself on my own cell phone and feign an emergency. No good. I was giving serious consideration to faking an epileptic seizure when I remembered that she was a doctor, and this was a doctor's office. I would be rushed to where I am right now and forced into a paper dress anyway.

I removed my clothes and hid my prosthetic penis in the pocket of my leather coat.

I was a coward in a paper dress, and it was cold in there.

She returned, looking chipper and self-assured, as I imagined it would be easy to feel when you are twenty-one and already a doctor. Where do I know her from? Think, man, think.

She checked my pulse, heart rate, felt my breasts. My mind raced, sketching one humiliating scenario after another.

I wake up with a cute girl in a shared east end house. We are smiling at each other over coffees when my doctor walks into the kitchen in her boxers and retrieves the orange juice from the refrigerator.

"Oh, Ivan, this is my roommate, the doctor."

The doctor winks at me and drinks from the carton. "We've met. As a matter of fact, under all those shirts, Ivan has quite a nice rack, dontcha Iv'?"

You see, this is the curse a writer must live with everyday of their life. An imagination. It's not all hot cars and fast women. I have to live inside this head. All alone, on a good day.

"So . . . just scootch your butt down to the end of the table, and put your feet into these little foot things, so your vagina is right on the edge here."

She said vagina. In reference to myself. I couldn't believe she said vagina. And isn't there a technical term for those little foot things? I was shocked by her casual bedside manner. I was about to undergo a rather traumatic medical procedure here, wearing a paper dress, no less, and she was acting like we were changing a carburetor together. And where have I met her before?

My heart was pounding, every ounce of my flesh fighting with my brain which was screaming, run boy, while you still can, while you still have the strength, no one's gonna blame you, she said vagina. . . .

I heard the snap of a latex glove, and may have lost consciousness at that point for a moment, I'm not sure.

From outside my body I could see myself standing at the bar, bad music pounding, and the doctor talking to a group of girls with nose rings, gesturing at me with her beer. "That Ivan sure has a healthy looking cervix."

"You might feel a slight pinch, we need a little tissue sample, there you go, it's all over, until next year."

She snapped off her glove and threw it into the little garbage can. "So. . . ." she rubs her cold hands together. "We've missed you at hockey the last couple of months. You been working too much?"

Weak Nine

At least this time I didn't feel like killing anyone.
They say that it only takes four days for the nicotine
to leave your system, that any craving beyond that is
purely psychological. I don't know who "they" are,
or if "they" ever found themselves at the business
end of a Player's Light Regular, because I've talked
to folks who quit ten years ago who still longingly
watch the orange glow in another's hand on its
peaceful rounds: mouth, lap, hip, little circles in the
air when they speak. I love watching someone
smoke in the dark.

I prepared this time: quit drinking coffee, bought
gum and cinnamon sticks. I avoided places and
activities which I would associate with smoking. I
found that it wasn't so bad, as long as I didn't work,
eat, drink, sleep, or have sex with anyone, I only
thought about cigarettes most of the time. But I
stuck it out.

One month later, pink-tongued and righteous, I
was overheard exclaiming that I would never smoke

again, that I didn't miss it a bit, this was it, I was so over it all. I believed I was cured.

When the guy in the basement suite of the house next door lit up, I could smell it, sharp-toothed and stagnant. I could tell a smoker from ten paces. "To think, I once smelled like that," I would say, like a born-again Christian, so convinced was I of my own salvation.

I had a dream that I was walking the empty hallways of my elementary school. I passed a classroom door that was open. Inside was a kindergarten class, thirty or so five-year-olds going about their kindergarten business, finger-painting and block-stacking and what not, all of them with cigarettes dangling from corners of their tiny mouths like construction workers. I stopped, and was staring, when a little boy walked up to the door.

"What the fuck are you looking at?" he asked me in his little boy's falsetto, ground out his butt with the heel of his blue and red sneaker, and slammed the door in my face.

Eight weeks gone, I carefully washed all the ashtrays in my house and stowed them away in a cupboard. I removed my silver lighter from my right front pocket and tucked it into a drawer.

Then I got drunk. Four scotches and two sweaty dances later, the tall blonde sipped her drink through a straw and offered me a smoke. Sure, why not? It's not like I'm still addicted or anything, besides, it's only a Du Maurier, how good can it be?

How good can it be. I had another one later, at her place, watching the smoke curl lazily around her long fingers and catch the streetlight seeping through her bedroom window.

Truth was, I never felt like a non-smoker. I was just a smoker who didn't. I wasn't ready to trade in my leather jacket for Gortex or fleece. I was tired of smelling good. I missed my nagging cough.

The guy at my corner store hadn't seen me in nine weeks. "I thought maybe you moved from the neighbourhood," he said as he took my six bucks and slid the blue and white package across the counter.

"No, I didn't leave, I just quit for a while." I said with resignation.

He smiled and shrugged his shoulders. "Maybe now it will be easier the next time, huh?"

That's what they say.

Stupid Man

I like the cheap produce, and the fresh flowers, and the Rice Dream (for guests), but mostly I shop there because of her attitude.

She single-handedly fights to fend off the stereo-type of the docile, soft-spoken Chinese woman behind the counter. I see her on the front lines for everyone, heating up samosas and sliding packs of Player's Lights and setting an example for all of us.

I went in one night for cigarettes, and asked her how she was doing, more out of good manners than conversation, but she told me the truth; few ever do.

"I ask you now, what time is it? A quarter after nine o'clock? The only thing I ask my husband is for Tuesday nights I watch a – how do you say – Chinese soap opera? He is supposed to come here at eight o'clock, so where is he at? And where are my friends? Waiting outside my house maybe? I don't know, I am stuck here all night. And then some fucking guy, he just stole a whole box of Oreo cookie ice cream sandwiches, so I ask you, what kind of a life is this?"

I took my cigarettes and left meekly. I was almost afraid to ask her how she was the next time I went in. When you ask someone how they are doing, you rarely expect them to actually tell you how they are doing.

A couple of weeks later I went in on a Friday night to pick up a few things for breakfast the next day. Never being one to shy away from the truth, I asked her, "How's it going?"

Her eyes flashed hard and sharp, and she snapped her answer back at me, her head jerking towards the back of the store: "Why don't you ask stupid man how am I doing?"

Her husband had his back turned towards us, quietly pricing cans of coconut milk; his wide shoulders slumped inward. I went to get some crackers and he met my eyes, nodded hello, and looked back down.

"What's up with her?" I asked him. "Good thing you can get a deal on flowers, huh?"

He smiled weakly, like January sun, and cleared his throat and spoke, quietly. "I was in the back, and I hear her scream that we're being robbed, so I come running out to see a tall, skinny, white man running out the door. I chase him up to Twelfth Avenue, and across the traffic and down past the Mohawk. I jumped him on the grass by the apartment, and he rolls over on his back and says: 'Don't hurt me don't hurt me I'm sorry, here is your orange juice, here take it back,' so I give him one kick in the ass and let him go. He runs away. I come back here and give her back the orange juice."

"And she's mad at you? She didn't even say thank you?"

He shakes his head like a wet husky and motions for us to lower our voices. "No, all she said is: 'Very good, there is my orange juice. Now where is my eight hundred and fifty dollars?' She didn't tell me he took the money from the till, too."

I managed to wait until I got in the car to start laughing at him. *Why don't you ask stupid man how I'm doing?* Not that robbery is funny at all. I myself lost all my CDs (again) the night before last; theft in the East End is never funny. None of us have insurance.

It's just that her husband is a black belt, could have killed the guy, and chose not to. He is a gentle man, great with produce, fresh flowers, sweet to his two daughters. Next time they get robbed, he should call in the heavy artillery. Next time he should send his wife.

Older Women

He has the nicest yard on the block. Ours has the tallest sunflowers, and the lilacs, but the old guy on the corner has the time to really prune his shrubs. His grass is always cut golf green short, he has one of those ice cream cone flowering trees and wisteria vines around his windows, and cherry trees, both pink and white in spring. He also has the veggie plot, with tomatoes in rows like soldiers and beans at attention, tied up with bits of blue jerrycloth towels. Even his broccoli looks organized.

He was a tough nut to crack. I've lived here two houses down the block from him for nine and a half years now, and he only started to like me last January, when I bought a Ford Taurus station-wagon just like the one he has, except his is white.

I was okay enough to nod at before, when I drove the beat-up van, mostly because we kept the yard and he saw us leaving for work early in the morning and dutifully walking our dogs at night, but in eight years he never actually spoke to me until the Taurus.

His wife had always chatted over the fence to everyone when he wasn't around, but she had passed on about two years ago. I remember the red lights swirling on my wall and ceiling when the ambulance came, and how he kept all the blinds down for a couple of months after she was gone, and for a while there were all these cars parked on the street outside with Ontario and Alberta plates.

"Nice looking car. Good shape. Good car. She a '93?" He was letting his old, almost blind and deaf shepherd out for a stretch.

I nodded. "It's not the sexiest ride, but I travel a lot. I can still sleep in the back, room for the dogs. I still miss my Valiant."

He scoffed and shook his head. "That piece of garbage, I wanted to throttle you some mornings, listening to you trying to get that thing started. Getting where you're going on time is sexy. You get a little bit older, son, gas mileage will become what is sexy. You did a smart thing, to buy yourself a decent car for once."

Son? No wonder he didn't talk to me for nine years. He thought there was a sixteen-year-old boy living next door with no apparent parental guidance all this time. He was probably concerned for his car stereo and the tools in his garage.

Soon thereafter he started to salute me whenever he saw me, fan rake at his side, as I walked by on my way to the park or unloaded my groceries. We started to bitch about people who never adhered to the playground speed limit, and how crazy drivers would never slow down to let even baby carriages or strings of ducklings cross safely these days. Last month he gave me a Safeway bag full of pears from his tree when I walked past with the dogs. I gave him a jar of peaches my aunt sent down for my birthday. An exchange of fruit seemed in order.

Last week my girlfriend from Montana was in town. I introduced her to Anton when we were all dressed up and getting in the car to go out for dinner. She was wearing a velvet dress and tall black boots. Anton made exaggerated movements above his head, like he was doffing an imaginary feathered cap, and bowed deeply to her from his side of the chain link fence. "A pleasure, miss. Have a lovely evening, you two." He winked approvingly at me as I opened the car door for her, and smiled and waved as we drove off.

The next time I walked by he motioned me over to the fence conspiratorially. "Come, come," he whispered. He seemed excited, and there was a spark in his watery eyes. "She is beautiful." He smiled widely, his chest and arms still powerful under his cardigan and grey t-shirt. "She is maybe a little older than you, no?"

I shrugged and smirked back at him, saying

nothing.

"You realize a woman's love is like a fly?" He raised an eyebrow at me. "And just like a fly, her love is just as likely to land on a pile of shit as it is a rose." He took out his hanky, blew his nose, and stuffed it into the front pocket of his trousers. "What I mean is, don't ask yourself why a beautiful girl might love you, just be glad she picked you to love. It's good to love a girl older than you, in the long run it is like your old Valiant: if it is too young and beautiful, you may or may not ever get where you are going, and besides, what has it cost you to get there? The shirt off your back, that's what, young man, that's what. Comprendes?"

I didn't really get what Anton was saying, but I could tell that it was important to him that I did, so I nodded.

"You know my Camilla was ten years older than me? My only sadness, my single regret, is that she is without me now, for a while, up in heaven." Anton crossed himself, and I followed, as taught by my grandmother. He went on. "There never was a better wife for me than Camilla. I never worried where Camilla was. If she had been ten years younger, maybe it would be a different story, you see? It is a smart young man who marries an older woman."

Anton held up one finger for me to wait a moment, and he shuffled up his back stairs into his pantry off the kitchen. He came back with a jar of stewed tomatoes. "Camilla canned these. You take them; it's one of the last jars I have. You cook a nice meal for that girl; she is a real catch, and I watched how she looked at you. She loves you, and you are a lucky man for it. You cook for her, you hear me? I've watched them come and go over the years. This girl, there is something about her. She has a kind of grace; my Camilla, she had it too."

This was the most Anton had ever said to me all at one go, and his eyes were tearing up. He fumbled for his hanky with one hand and shooed me off home with his other. "And wash your damned car. It's covered in mud. You take care of it. It's a good car."

Fish Stories

I don't know why I love fish stories, but I love fish stories. The one that got away, the one that didn't, how big it was and how feisty, and how you cooked it and how everyone said it was the best they ever had. And I love fishing, that combination of true relaxation and every-cast-could-land-you-a-big-one excitement known only to the angler. I love how your sweater smells like campfire and fish blood and lake water and wind when you get home, and after all that, you get to come home and tell fish stories.

So they call him Joe Fish, although I don't believe that is his legal name, Joe Fish is what they call him, on account of how much he loves to fish. I met him telling fish stories in that little corner store-sandwich bar place under the Skytrain cut, between the Vietnamese hair salon and the drop-off laundry place. An unlikely strip in an unlikely spot, it is where I most like to drink coffee. Even though the proprietor refuses to get an espresso machine (he maintains it keeps the film guys from coming in), it is my drip coffee hang-out of choice, mostly on account of the old men and their fish stories.

Fish stories are not always only about fish, you see.

Joe Fish is a soul fisherman, like I was when I was a little gaffer. Rain or shine, war or peace, starving or stuffed; any fishing is better than none. By the time most of our alarm clocks go off he is on his way back into town with the catch of the day, just on time to drop by the old sandwich bar for a bowl of tomato vegetable and black coffee with Sweet 'n' Low, and a few fish stories.

Joe and I, we're the morning crowd. 'Round about coffee time, the male nurses who work at the old folks home next door all parade in for BLTs and a few quick smokes and the talk turns maybe to politics, or taxes, or what a freak George Dubya is, how his eyes are too close together like some kind of warthog or something, and that's about when Roger the Rascally Rabbit shows up. At first I didn't know why a seventy-nine-year-old man would land a nickname like that, but then I sat next to him at the sandwich bar, and we got to telling Roger's version of fish stories. Roger has shrapnel in his head and his right hip, and the pills take care of the grand mal seizures he gets since he fought in Korea, but he gets these little ones, smells weird things, gets fuddled up, but not since he started smoking pot.

"Here I am," he says, pulling out two baggies

from the Compassion Club, "with a half-ounce of medical grade weed in my pocket, and all I feel like doing is popping home for a shot of rye. Go figure."

Roger the Rascally Rabbit used to be an electrician. He has outlived both of his children and his marriage. Fish stories.

The other day, Joe Fish brings in this buddy of his. I had just got back from the Yukon and had some new fish stories of my own, and so we all get to talking. Joe's buddy is named Mike, he's seventy-eight and looks maybe sixty, a real spry fella. I told them I was on my way back from camping in Squamish, where the Chinooks are running.

"Which river?" Mike asks. "The Cheakamus or the Chuckanut?" Mike knows the country. Paradise Valley. He figures I'm okay, he likes me all right, I know his stomping grounds.

"The best whore that ever worked in Squamish lives out near there," Mike says. "I should take you to meet her. She's retired now, but she still makes the best apple pie I ever had, and I always really had a soft spot saved for her. A real good ol' gal." He winks at me. I think he thinks I'm a young guy, but I'm not sure. I smile and wink back, sincerely, thinking of all the whores I've loved, and we drink coffee in silence for a while. Mike is looking kinda sentimental, so I have to ask him.

"What was her name, Mike? The best whore

that ever worked in Squamish, what was her name?"

Mike wrinkles his nose and shakes his head slowly. "You know, I cannot for the life of me remember her name. That's the thing about getting old that fools you: you think you're only going to forget stuff that doesn't really matter, but that's not what happens at all. You just forget."

Jeff the owner jumps up and unplugs something, just as Connie the Junkie comes in for smokes. She goes over to the pay phone, picks it up, listens, slams it back down. "Jeezus, when they gonna come fix this thing?"

Jeff shrugs sympathetically. "I called 'em, told 'em it's broke, but who knows with those guys."

Connie leaves. Jeff plugs the pay phone back in again. "I feel bad, but I can't have her sitting on the edge of my sandwich counter doing business."

"You are perfectly right. A fella can't eat his sandwich with that kind of activity sat right down beside you." Roger the Rascally Rabbit is shocked by Connie and her scabby legs and bruises, as are we all. "She should know better. This is a family establishment we got ourselves here."

We all nod into our styrofoam cups, watch the traffic. Tell stories.

THERE

Trick Road Trip

It's not just the leopard skin fun fur. No, it's not just that. Bed in the back attack, four inches of foam under your dome kick back, four speakers, and no lack of foot room. Four doors, too, and genuine pine tongue-in-groove ceiling, say what, tongue-in-groove ceiling, it's what they call custom-fitted for comfort. I've got Christmas lights on the dash that run off of AAs, a CD player, and a red bean bag ashtray. Oh yeah.

Number 99 southbound. Please remove sunglasses when driving through tunnel. If you leave leftover Chinese food on the engine cover, it will be warm by the time you get stuck in traffic. It is the art of the road trip and this is what you call a nuance. A fundamental being the company you keep.

Riding at my side is the naughtiest pretty boy I know, with a fresh haircut and eyelashes that should be illegal. Stacked boots and brand new blue jeans that bulge in all the right directions. I never could resist a lad like that; I would have made a terrible lesbian.

Aretha reminds me of Gil Scott-Heron because the revolution will not be televised which reminds me to put on television, the drug of a nation, breeding ignorance and feeding radiation and the Disposable Heroes take us through the border where we are greeted by a boy scout who welcomes us to America and makes sure we have enough ice and rolling papers. "Remember to ensure that your campfires are properly put out." He salutes us and we pull out for Bellingham.

There's an exit in the pass, I don't know the number but I could show you, and at the Texaco station is an espresso and sandwich bar manned by a shorn-headed angel who offers you three kinds of cheese if you have short hair like hers, if you know what I mean, so we fill up and let the dog out for a pee.

There is not a cloud in the sky and pine trees line the highway, the sun strobes between them as we sail past exit seventy-five and still alive, damn this thing runs fucking great since I switched to high octane.

There's a place called Friday Creek that marks halfway from Vancouver to Seattle and we change the CD to commemorate its passing. I still believe in Dr Hook. I started in my dad's '49 Ford when I was five, and why stop now? I'm not a bad person, I don't drink and I don't kill, I got no evil habits, and I probably never will, please, now don't misunderstand me, it's not love I'm tryin' to buy, it's just I got all this here money, and I'm a pretty ugly guy . . . but I got more money than a horse has hair, cuz my rich old uncle died, and answered all my prayers. . . .

Nathan and I decide to do a big drag number to honour the time-worn brilliance of Dr Hook and then flip to kd lang's version of Steve Miller's "The Joker" because we're nearing Seattle and I'm thinking of peaches. We call ahead to make sure she's ready.

I think that I shall never see a poem as lovely as her peaches, abundant and too much for one hand and she is packed and waiting, sparkling on her sidewalk in the sun. She always stops my breath like that, the first time every time, it's like that with me and her. She has cooked potato salad and made iced tea and we throw it in the cooler. She slips me a little tongue and takes the back seat.

We have sleeping bags and flashlights and a blow-up raft and fishing rods and a propane heater, and we are headed for the desert. It is high noon Easter morning and the whole world is a cherry blossom.

Life was almost perfect, until yesterday when I found a black polyester shirt with yellow and red sparkly flames all over it, and now it is sublime.

I have never seen the Grand Canyon, purple

mountain majesty, and I need to hear the artist formerly known as because she reminds me of something James used to say: I like 'em fat, and I like 'em proud, you got to have a mother for me so move your big ass 'round this way, so I can work on that zipper baby, cuz tonight, you're a star, and I'm the big dipper.

Nathan stretches, puts his new boots on the dash, and winks at a trucker as we drive out of his shadow. I smile at her in the rearview mirror. She is tinted afternoon orange by this four o'clock light. Looks like we'll be in Portland in time to watch the sun go down on all those bridges.

Leave It to Beaver

How many trips up this highway? The bliss that pumps in my blood the moment my wheels turn towards home, how my heart smiles when the pavement turns to chipseal turns to gravel.

It is my ritual, the bringing down of the cooler, the shaking out of the sleeping bags. How do the dogs know? They don't wait by the door like this when I clean out the closet or gather the laundry.

They must know we're headed north.

I never need much of a reason to go home. This time it was just a postcard.

"I've got the camper fixed up and the truck is tuned and ready to go," my grandmother wrote in her perfect, old-lady script. "If you don't come up and go camping with me soon, we'll regret it for the rest of our lives. Or should I say, *you'll* regret it for the rest of *your* life."

Once a Catholic, always primed for a guilt trip. I checked the calendar, and the bank account. I'd have to be back in two and a half weeks: four days home, four days back. A little over a week there. If I could find my Louis L'Amour books on tape, I could be on the road by four o'clock.

This is why I don't keep houseplants.

I stopped briefly in the low brush just outside Hope to pick some sage for the dash. Smells great when you turn on the heater in the morning. Avocado and asiago cheese sandwich on rye bread, and mandarin juice in a can. I let the dogs out. The husky does some calisthenics and yawns, sniffs around my feet for crumbs; the little guy chases mosquitoes. The city is just an unnatural glow in the sky behind us.

We hit the road as soon as the kinks are stretched out of my legs. I was pushing to make it just past Williams Lake, to my secret camping spot. Last time, orange surveyor's tape was wrapped around the trees in the clearing, and the road had been widened, but I was hoping it hadn't changed yet. I wanted to wake up next to a lonesome sparkling lake and the sound of loons.

I was up just before dawn; the dogs were barking. The windows were fogged up, but I could still see her and her baby before they lumbered into the brush. Bears. Good thing I decided against pitching the tent in the dark. There was frost on the windshield and a thin frozen film in the dog water. I figured I'd stop for coffee somewhere else.

Early September is the best time to hit the Alaska Highway. Most of the motorhomes have turned around to take the grandkids back to school, and you can still beat the night.

You leave Vancouver in late summer. You drive ten or twelve hours a day for four days. The days get longer the further north you go. If you haul ass as the day is waning, you can chase the light; that is, you can drive through an extended sunset, one that happens longer for you in your moving car than it does for any stationary person watching from the back deck. In September, the sky is still orange in Fort St John long after the porch lights have come on in Prince George. Autumn is a fast-forward blur of yellow poplars and emergency orange birch trees. You don't watch the leaves fall, you drive to a place where they're already gone.

I started to get sleepy the third afternoon. Nina Simone and the smell of sage lulled me into the willows, the road a dusty zipper up the belly of a sleeping, tree-covered beast. I pulled into a campground, crawled into the back, and crashed.

I woke up to the smell of wood smoke, and stumbled out, fuzz-mouthed, into my little campsite.

"Whatcha git me for my birthday?" She was gravel-voiced and full of belly laughs.

I spun around to see who had spoken. Much had happened during my two-hour nap. The campsite next to me now held a dilapidated trailer that looked like it couldn't take one more move, and she was parked on a faded lawn chair beside it. "I said, where is my birthday present, sonny?"

She was talking to me, her brown eyes sparkling above raisin-wrinkled cheeks and beneath silver braids. Her legs were spread wide to make room for her belly, and she had two wooden canes slung over the arm of her lawn chair. She spat tobacco juice through the hole where her two front teeth had been and winked at me.

"So how old are you?" I asked, because it seemed the obvious thing.

She was waiting for it. "I am eighty-two years old. So whatcha bring me?" She laughed and coughed, and slapped her knee. "Come have a beer with me. Bring my present."

I grabbed my penny whistle out of the bag on the front seat. "I didn't buy you anything this year – I mean, what do you get the woman who has everything?" I gestured around us, to the muddy river, the spindly pines, and the smoking campfire. "So I wrote you a song."

I played her a jig, or maybe it was a reel, I can

never tell the difference, and she heaved herself out of the lawn chair, planted one cane in the dust and jigged (or was it reeled?) herself in a circle with the other cane. Her tongue stuck out of one corner of her smile, and we kind of hop-danced together like that for a while, until the dust rose around us and beads of sweat popped in the maze of lines on her forehead.

She collapsed back into her squealing lawn chair, still laughing from down in her belly, and motioned to the chair next to her. "Richie, get this" – she narrowed a wizened gaze at my chest, then up to my throat – "new friend of mine a beer, would ya? Make yerself useful. My name is Rosie. Everyone calls me Grandma." She banged on the door of the trailer with the worn rubber tip of her cane. "Richie, you gone deaf in there?"

A scruffy looking fellow in his late twenties shuffled out of the trailer with a Budweiser for me. "Hey, I'm Richard." He extended his hand tentatively, like he didn't expect anyone would actually shake it, his head cocked a little to one side.

"Thanks, but no." I took his hand in mine, and left the beer. "I've got to drive."

"So what?" they both said in unison.

"It's only American beer," Grandma added, a frown gathering around her mouth. "Have a beer with an old lady on her birthday. Maybe it's my last. Who knows, eh?"

Rosie and my grandmother should get together. They could talk me into anything.

Halfway through my warm Budweiser, a primer-coloured truck belched into the campground and backed into Rosie's little driveway, a load of firewood heaped so high I couldn't see who was in the front seat, until they came piling out.

A stocky man jumped from the driver's side and began directing the swarm of youngsters where to stack the firewood. He lit a smoke and strutted over to Rosie, kissed her cheek.

"Happy birthday, Mum. Richie, get up off your ass and get your father a beer. I'm Dennis," he said curtly to me, raising his cowboy hat. Dennis sported a Mack Truck belt buckle and veins wrapped around his forearms like ropes. Amazingly white teeth shone like a billboard in the middle of his brown face. "You got a name?"

"Yeah, sorry . . . I'm Ivan."

Dennis snorted, looked me up and down, cracked his beer with the thumb of the hand he held it in, and turned his gaze to his son. "This your new girlfriend, Richie?"

Richard swallowed, looked down, and said nothing.

"You from down south then?" Dennis leaned back on the heels of his boots and squinted at the license plate on my car.

I shook my head. "I'm from Whitehorse. I live in Vancouver now, but I was born and raised up North." Guys like Dennis don't like city types too much.

Dennis raised his eyebrow and looked at me again. Ironically, I too, am wearing a big brass Snap-on Tools belt buckle, cowboy hat, and work boots.

"What's your dad do?" he actually looked me in the eye this time. This was code for *Are you one of us or not?*

"He's a welder. Does a lot of work for truckers. He builds aluminum boats, too." I let a little pride slip into my voice. My dad can build anything. Nothing's broken that he can't fix.

Dennis nodded. Richard jumped up, made a beeline for the trailer, then came back with an army green backpack, and reached deep inside.

"I'm starting a carpentry apprenticeship this fall. Going to Edmonton for school. I made Grandma a coffee table, she says you can't tell it from one you buy in a store, right Gran? Here, I'll show you, I made this." His slender hand came out of the back-pack with a small treasure which he handed to me.

It was a wooden knot cut from a piece of pine tree, about the size of an egg. It had been hollowed out and a smooth cut piece of the bottom of a beer bottle painstakingly fitted into the hole. Etched carefully in an arc around the hole were the words

FORGET ME KNOT in bold block letters. I turned it over in my palm. It had been carefully sanded and varnished.

"See, here, I'll show you." Richard grabbed it back from me, excited like a kid. He held it like a telescope up to one eye, and squinted the other one closed. "It changes how you see everything. Like rose-coloured glasses." He gave it back, making a go-ahead-try-it motion with both hands.

I looked through it. The world was an amber-coloured shoplifting mirror. I nodded in apprecia-tion, and Richard's grin split his face.

"Tell her where you learned to make that, Richie. Go on, tell her. Where'd you learn to build things?"

His father's voice caused Richard's shoulders to fall back towards each other, and he went silent.

Dennis answered his own question. "Two to five for armed robbery, that's where, ain't that right? Didn't even make any money at it, did'ja, who else would be so dumb to rob a fucking gardening store in October?" He spat in the dust and shook his head.

"Leave the boy, Dennis." Rosie lifted one cane in her son's direction. "Nobody is perfect, right, Don Juan? Should we tell our new friend where your third wife is? Or how 'bout you explain how you got that scar in your eyebrow?" Rosie stared with soft eyes at her son and grandson.

Dennis returned her stare for a second, then

looked at his boots, took a long pull on his Budweiser, and ran the back of his hand across his mouth.

"Jesus H for the love of . . . get that thing off the fire." The kindness was gone from the old woman's voice, and she scrambled to pull herself to her feet. "Did God put a brain in your head? Move it!"

For the first time, I noticed the carcass suspended over the little campfire. Nephews and cousins scurried to find sticks strong enough to lift it off the Y-shaped poles and over to the picnic table. It was a skinless, smallish animal, unrecognizable enough without its pelt, even more so now that it had caught fire and was enveloped in a ball of black smoke and flaming fat. After much swearing and tripping and running amok, eventually someone threw a wet dishcloth over it and put it out.

Rosie sat back into her lawn chair, out of breath from screaming orders and reprimands. "Let it cool off a bit, the inside bits will still be okay. A bit of burnt never killed anyone." She turned to me. "The grandkids bagged a beaver this afternoon."

I nodded, of course. Of course that was a beaver that just caught on fire. What else? I was starting to really like these guys. They made my family look normal.

Richard passed me another beer. "Tastes like chicken, I think. You ever eaten beaver?"

Rosie snorted so loud it sounded like it hurt, and

choked a bit on her beer. "My god boy, maybe you
are stupid. Look at her. What do you think? Looks
like a beaver eater if I ever saw one." She rocked
back and slapped both knees, and laughed until
tears ran.

Dennis smirked. I smiled. Richard looked confused. One of the grandkids interrupted this magic
moment buy slicing the better part of his left thumb
off with his jack knife, and I took the opportunity to
pour the rest of my beer out while everyone was
distracted by talk of stitches and where the first aid
kit was.

I followed Dennis's truck out of the campground. I could see his cowboy hat move as he
leaned over to put his arm around the injured boy.
Rosie waved from her lawn chair, and Richard ran
up beside my car and pressed the forget-me-knot
into my palm.

Dust rose in a cloud behind the pick up and
ground between my teeth. I couldn't tune in a radio
station; the digital numbers just rolled on and on, no
signal to be found. It was eight o'clock and the sun
still hung orange above the horizon, not on its way
anywhere for a while yet.

It was good to be home.

More Beautiful

"There is for sure more beautiful canyons out there," he told us. "But none *that* big. I mean, it really is a *grand* canyon."

We were in the Powell Lake campground in Arizona and I had finally figured out why he was being so friendly. We were writing in our journals by candlelight the first time he came up to our picnic table. He had appeared, a shadow at first, backlit by the RV lights behind him, gas lantern in hand.

"You ladies wanna borrow this?" He held up the hissing light.

"We're okay with the candles, thanks."

He shrugged, as if to say "suit yourself," and went back to his side of the white stake that marked our site.

"You doin' any fishing?" He had a white ice cream bucket with him this time. "You gotta try anchovies. Fresh ones, that is. Be careful, though, they got laws now, no live bait, but everybody does it." He gestured plaintively with his bucket of fish. "You wanna take a few?"

I shook my head thanks but no thanks. "We're going to the canyon tomorrow. Won't be fishing for a couple of days."

"Me and the wife just came from there, the North Rim, though, it's less populated. She doesn't like the crowds much." He shrugged again. "She's in town right now, doing some shopping. Just dropped me off. Left my keys in the dash. I'm locked out of the trailer till she gets back, I guess. I'm s'posed to start the pork chops, too."

That's why he keeps coming over here. He was hungry. "Well, pull up a picnic table, and pour yourself a coffee." We both spring up to move things around and make room for the poor bastard. He was lost without her. "There's more noodles and stuff."

He looked relieved, and helped himself, talking through mouthfuls. "You gotta go at least once, just to see the thing. But go to the North Rim. Less tourists, if you know what I mean."

After he finished the leftovers, he showed us how to get there on the coffee-stained map. "That there is quite the mountain pass. You'll want to get an early start, before the day heats up too much."

It was like leaving one theme room for another, the way the desert and dry road dust gave way to a quick climbing mountain road and lush pines and wildflowers, and the car groaned at the heat and hill under us and up we climbed.

Jacobs Lake was the turnoff for the North Rim access to the Grand Canyon, and it was nine miles ahead. We were nine thousand feet above sea level when the fuel pump gave up the ghost as we rounded a bend and the car stalled to a stop in the gravel.

I took off my cowboy hat, licked my fingers to smooth down my camping hair, and stuck my thumb out. A guy named Bob and his son, Bobby Junior, picked me up in a haywired-together Chevy. Bobby Junior gave me half his turkey sandwich, and they dumped me off outside a faded Texaco.

"Sounds like a fuel pump to me," the mechanic talked around the toothpick in his mouth and didn't stop squinting when he walked out of the sun into the service bay. "And if you're going to have fuel system problems, you'll have them at nine thousand feet for sure. That hill kills more fuel pumps. . . ." He dialed the rotary phone with a dirt-worn-in finger. "Can't fix it here, we only do tires." He owned the only gas station, the only campground, and the only pay phone, which was out of order. "I'll call Nick Ramsey in Kanab. He's got the only tow truck around. He's got a shop there, too, 'bout forty miles thataway."

"Is he Triple A?" I mean, that's why you pay into these things, for emergencies like this. He nodded and handed me the phone.

The tow truck driver's name was JD, and he loaded us up onto his flatbed truck and off we went. We never once slowed to under eighty miles an hour, and I white-knuckled it all the way down the other side of the pass, as JD explained to us that he wasn't just a mechanic, he was taking criminology at night school, and he was trying to get into the FBI. I watched his sausage-fingered hands pass over each other as he double-clutch shifted and smoked and answered his cell phone and played with the radio all at the same time as we careened into town.

We pulled up to a clean and newer looking service station right on the main strip on the leaving town side of the highway.

A skinny-looking guy with no grease under his nails came out, wiping his clean hands on a clean rag. Skinny guy was the not-so-mechanical second son of Nick Ramsey, the guy who owned this brand new station, and its fleet of butch and shiny tow trucks.

"That'll be a hunnerd and eighty bucks," skinny guy said, with his chin jutting out towards me.

I whipped out my BCAA card.

He shook his head. "Don't do Triple A tows. Hunnerd and eighty bucks." He planted both feet in the red dust and surveyed my car, still six feet off the ground on the back of the flatbed. "Cash or credit."

I paid him for the tow in cash; what could I do? JD lowered my car to the ground, unhooked the chains, an unlit smoke dangling from the corner of his mouth. "Leo in Jacob's Lake says he figures it sounds like a fuel pump. We'll know in a minute. It's the altitude. Ten bucks says she'll turn over just fine now we're down the mountain."

JD was right, my car started and ran fine. We could take our chances and hightail it out on a different highway, or we could get the car fixed and finally see the Grand Canyon.

Skinny guy looked at his watch and explained that it was the May long weekend and that theirs was the only shop in town open at all on the weekends and plus his family owned the only auto parts place, and that it was past six but that his brother or his dad would come in tomorrow and fix it, but it would cost me double-time on account of the holiday. I really didn't like this guy and said I'd think about it.

"What's to think about? You getting your car fixed or what?" he called out as I drove away.

There is always more than one mechanic in town, I know that much. Plus, you should never believe the guy who just ripped you off once already.

Sure enough, at the Chevron up the street a guy in coveralls stood smoking a cigarette and kicking the tires of an old car with another fella.

"Fuel pump went on the pass, had to get towed here," I explained.

"Nick Ramsey didn't tow you in, did he?"

I nodded. "Unfortunately, yes, he did."

"He didn't pull his Triple A scam on you, did he?" The guy in coveralls winced. "I hate it when he does that." He shook his head sadly. "We got a truck, too, plus we're Triple A. Wait'll my boss hears they're up to it again over there. Chamber of Commerce already wrote 'em up for it, but he thinks he can do as he pleases, on account of how he's Nick Ramsey. His old man owned half this town, left it all to him. We're not all like that . . . Mormons, that is."

They fixed the car for us the very next morning; the owner himself drove nine miles to the next town for the part. They all felt sorry for the poor Canadian girls and gave us free coffee and camping advice.

It was while we were drinking those coffees that the road trip gods smiled upon us so brightly that it even made up for the fuel pump. We started talking to these hippie juice squeezers who had a lemon yellow plywood stand beside the highway, offering beet and garlic juice and orange carrot juice and everything. She was really a folk singer and he was a rock-climber and they told us about a secret access road, known only to the locals, an almost unused dirt road into the Toroweep viewpoint of the Grand Canyon. A solitary view 3,600 feet down the canyon to the mighty Colorado.

After the fuel pump was fixed, we loaded up on gas and water, followed the highway back through town, turned right on a secondary highway, and took a left at the cow bridge. This is about where we could have used a four-wheel drive vehicle of some sort, or at least something with more clearance than a Ford Taurus station wagon. But if you drive fast over the washboard and slow between pot-holes and over jutting rocks, even a Taurus will take you there. We were worried about flats – we had already found out just how much a tow truck could set you back in these parts, but we didn't even talk about turning around.

I'm not going to let slip more specific directions, other than the clues I've already given above. It's one of those places you've got to find in order to deserve to see it. At the end of the sixty-two-mile-long car-beating road was a definitely no-frills campground. It was a good thing we had lots of water, and a garbage bag, because there wasn't even a trash can. There was nothing but a biffy and three tent sites. The non-descript sage and desert landscape gave way to low shrubs and desert wildflowers, then cactus, and then the rocks began to change, and we could feel it long before the road got there. The Grand Canyon. The best tent site was literally twenty feet from the edge of the canyon. There were no guardrails, no concrete, no tour buses. The most visited national treasure in all of the U.S., and we spent it alone, save for the biker and his wife, and a young man escorting an old lady and her watercolours.

We stayed until we started to run out of Marlborough Lights and fresh water, marveling over little blue-green lizards and the strange pull of a very big cliff just past the tips of your toes. My friend claimed she woke up several times a night with vertigo, her heart pounding with the gravity of it all. Me, I dreamt of wind and the smell of sheets fresh off the clothesline.

Fear of Hoping in Las Vegas

To tell you the honest truth, I had never really considered marriage until that night in the taco shop.

She had a veggie special burrito and I was working on a chicken supremo. You can eat for very little in San Francisco, provided you like beans and rice.

It was day four of my favourite kind of road trip, the kind where you find out where you're going when you get there, and we had a tablecloth made of road maps.

"I have always wanted to go to Death Valley," I confessed to her. The van was running great, we both liked the taste of back roads, even the city smelled like good luck.

"Sure, Death Valley sounds sexy, but I want to go to Vegas first."

"Vegas?" I raised an eyebrow. She didn't seem like the bright lights, big city type to me. We had slept in cemeteries and junkyards all the way down, she drank green tea and cracked organic black peppercorns onto my sandwiches with her teeth. She advocated the use of natural menstrual sponges. She and I in Las Vegas? I couldn't see it.

"Yeah, Vegas. I want to get married." Sour cream dripped off her little finger and landed on the Oregon coast.

"Who you gonna marry?" I passed her a napkin and folded up the sticky road map.

"*You*, you bonehead. Will you marry me?" She licked her fingers.

Now, perhaps I should have thought a bit at this juncture, maybe about things like commitment and vows and responsible behaviour and what-not, but thinking is contrary to the whole spirit of eloping, so I didn't. Think, that is.

"You want to think about it?" She asked me this, because she had proposed, time had elapsed, I was sitting open-mouthed, and had not answered.

"No – I mean yes, I mean sure, let's go to Las Vegas." My mouth moved with a mind of its own.

At high noon the next day the desert was dry-brushed sage and dust. The only things painted vivid were the tiny flowers on the cacti, the colour of purple that teenagers like to paint their toenails.

We were fifty miles outside of Las Vegas and I was searching for a sign. She was up in the hills behind me, taking photos, and I was praying for some guidance.

Okay, God, or whoever is responsible for these things, please give me a sign. Should we get married?

Heat waves were acid-tripping off bone-coloured sand, and quiet was everywhere. Nothing but the distant hum of the Interstate.

Then I saw an emerald green lizard skitter across the gravel and disappear.

Okay, God. Bright green lizards are really cool and all, but this is a monumental question here, I'm gonna need a big sign. Big as you can muster up, the kind I can't ignore. Hit me, Great Creator, to marry or not to marry?

I heard the grind of a tanker truck gearing down, and there it was. A sixteen wheeler painted painful white humped down the off-ramp and drove real slow, right past me. Stenciled on the side in block red letters was one word: LUCKY. And right behind that truck was another one, identical to the first. And then one more.

Three times lucky? Three times lucky! That settled it. Today was to be our wedding day.

My photographer fiancée came down from the hills smiling. "Take a picture," I laughed. "Take three pictures. It's a sign." My boots crunched gravel in a prenuptial dance. I dropped to my knees, grabbed a handful of wedding day dirt and tipped it into my pocket, for luck. "Let's go get married."

"Okay," she smiled again. "But it's my turn to drive."

The Strip in Las Vegas is a whirlwind of stimulation for a small town lad who doesn't play video games. I was glad she was driving. The first strip-mall we found had a tired little storefront that advertised free maps, colouring books, and wedding information. They're like that in Las Vegas.

The woman behind the counter had a face that looked like she smoked too much and wintered in Florida. I announced my marital intentions and she immediately sprang into a flurry of action. "How completely and utterly romantic. We have a number of lovely little chapels to pick from, here, take these brochures, and where is your lovely bride-to-be? She's out in the van? Well, go get her, son, let's have a look, isn't she beautiful? You two are going to make the most darling babies, here I'll just draw for you on the map the way to the courthouse, and the Candlelight Chapel, is it? An excellent choice, very quaint, they're all lovely people down there, they'll do something special for you, just tell them Karen sent you. Okay, let's call and book it for 7:45, shall we? Give you time to freshen up. Of course I need a seventy-five-dollar down payment, to book the chapel, you see, where did that receipt book disappear to?"

I was dazzled, and paid her in cash. She reached across the counter and stroked my cheek with the back of her hand. "You are a lucky bride," she said solemnly to my somewhat confused fiancée. "My Arnold had a baby face, too, that means he'll still be handsome in thirty years. God rest his soul. I miss him like he just went yesterday. Oh, to be like the two of you again. Best of luck to you. Make sure you send me a picture."

We left without mentioning that, biologically, I was female. It just didn't seem appropriate to spoil it all for Karen like that.

Only the bride and groom-to-be are allowed into the marriage license office. The hall outside the office was chaos, small children running amok and relatives of happy couples sweating in their Sunday best. We were ushered through a metal detector, my pocket knife was confiscated, and we got in line to wait.

All the other couples were staring at us. I presumed it was because I was wearing shining silver pants and a metallic blue cowboy hat with a dalmation fun-fur hat band, and she was stunningly beautiful. My palms began to sweat and for the first time I wondered how the State of Nevada really felt about same-sex marriages. But we had come so far. . . . I took out my driver's license. The only thing identifying me as female was a tiny capital F on the back. I removed some lucky wedding day dirt from my pocket and began to rub the grains of sand over the F with my thumb. It quite easily disappeared.

It seemed simple enough. I would just let her do the talking.

The woman behind the counter took our thirty-five dollars without a second glance. She filled out both our names on a form, and then a marriage certificate. Things were running smoothly, until she asked me what my middle initial, "E," stood for. My middle name is Elizabeth. This could prove somewhat problematic. "Uhh . . . Elliot." I had hesitated, and she looked up, her eyes narrowing.

"I'll be right back." She scooped up our IDs and paperwork, and disappeared into a back room with them.

She returned minutes later, accompanied by a woman with even bigger hair than hers, her supervisor. The supervisor came out from behind the counter and walked slowly around me, scrutinizing. I felt her eyes cross over my chest (I have no breasts to speak of, well, none that a good sports bra can't render harmless) and then down to my crotch. I was, as usual, packing. Still, she was on to me.

"Well, I am afraid I cannot issue you a marriage license. Both of you . . . appear to be female, and this identification," she paused to look over her spectacles at me, "appears to have been . . . tampered with. Two people of the same gender cannot be married in this state. I will thank you both to leave now."

The beefcake security guards didn't look too interested in hearing me pontificate about my theories refuting the binary gender system, they just pointed at the door.

We left, and as we walked past the gauntlet of staring couples, I felt something I thought I had grown out of: indignant rage. No fair no fair no fair! How come he can get married? He doesn't even look happy to be here. How come he can? He doesn't even have any teeth, and he's scoping out all the women except the one he is standing with. And how about him? He's wearing acid wash jeans, for chrissakes. The injustice of it all.

We walked back to the van. My ears burned, and my lovely bride-to-be placed a cool palm on the back of my neck. "We were so close. You just about gender-fucked the State of Nevada."

Any doubts I may have previously had were gone. This was Las Vegas. Someone was going to marry us. We were still booked at the Candlelight Chapel for 7:45.

"I'm afraid we can't perform a ceremony without a license here." He looked freshly scrubbed, and sincere. "I don't understand what the problem was, you're over eighteen, aren't you?" His desk in the chapel office was spotless and spit-shined. "Just try again. They change shifts every four hours, you'll probably get someone else, sir, and we can just move your booking ahead."

"I really don't think my age was the issue. Apparently two women cannot be wed, I think that's more the problem."

His jaw dropped, and again I felt his eyes: Adam's apple, chest, crotch. It was beginning to get tedious. "Well, then, we certainly can't marry you here, uhh . . . ma'am, we can't umm . . . help you at all."

He was nervous now. I had scrambled his sacred view of the world; I looked like a man but wasn't, and was probably dangerous. I asked him for our deposit back. "Well, I don't know anything about a deposit, you'll have to go back and talk to Karen about that." He moved things around on his desk, then moved them back.

Two ushers in tasteful blue suits were opening the oak doors out front. Both were sporting conspicuously new-looking wedding bands. One winked at us on our way out. "Best of luck to you, girls," he faux-lisped and gave us a limp-wristed salute. Apparently, when employed in Vegas, a wedding ring can be worn as part of a uniform.

I sat in the van and smoked, sadder than a sun-faded fun-fur skirt, while she went in and tried to get our deposit back. I watched her return empty-handed, the wind wrapping her dress around her thighs. "No dice, cowboy." She shrugged and climbed in. "Karen went home. It's a different woman, and she's not all that sympathetic."

I took the receipt from her. I was getting our money back. Starry-eyed lovers get ripped off in Las Vegas? Whoever heard of such a thing? "I'm gonna give it a try." I kissed her, and tasted tea tree oil and honey. "Cover me, I'm going in."

"And you must be the groom. I can see why they had trouble with you at the courthouse, you don't look a day over sixteen." She was older than Karen, with tired eyelids and lipstick escaping into the lines around her mouth. Her gold tag proclaimed her to be Rita. "I told your lovely bride, and I'm telling you, I can't give you your money back. Karen has it." Her voice sounded like gravel rolling over gravel. She was, as my grandmother would say, one tough cookie. This was going to take finesse.

"I'm not asking you for our money back. I just want you to find someone who will marry us without a license. Come on, Rita, just help us out."

"She pregnant? Is that what this is all about?" She looked at me sideways.

"No, nothing like that. We're in love."

"Love." She repeated, like she had finally heard it all. She took a deep breath and picked up the phone. "I want you to know this is coming out of my own pocket. Karen and I, we run a separate thing here. We're not partners, I just taught her everything she knows."

I imagined there wasn't much Rita couldn't teach.

"That you, Greg? Yup, it's me. Yah, he's fine, stitches come out on Thursday, ornery as ever, but what else is new . . . listen, can you marry a young couple I got here without a license? I dunno, some trouble down at the courthouse." She coughed and almost dropped the phone. "No . . . he's old enough." She looked at me like I was a shoplifter. "Well, it's hard to tell these days . . . he's wearing a cowboy hat."

I removed my hat and stood tall in front of her, palms up. "What do you need to see, Rita?" I was almost ready to give up.

"Yah, I gotta couple of ladies here for you, Greg, can you still do those? 'Kay, I'll send them right down."

Rita scribbled an address down for me, shaking her head. "They can take you at the Shamrock. You should have come clean with Karen in the first place. You got yourself into this, kiddo, you're lucky old Rita is helping you out at all. Bet Karen liked the looks of you though, huh?" She laughed, bringing on another cough. "She give you her line about Arnold? I taught her that line. Be careful out there; don't go getting yourself beat up now, you hear me?"

I thought I loved Karen, but I loved Rita more.

The Shamrock Wedding Chapel was located in the lobby of the Howard Johnson Hotel, just past the nickel slot machines. I went in alone; she stayed in the van to find some clean underwear and pick out a dress.

I had my vintage periwinkle blue suit with the velvet lapels slung over my forearm. The chapel was tiny, with a little office on the left, a couch, and a big screen TV in a little alcove on the right. Slumped on the couch was our reverend, his white collar half undone and his leftover belly arguing with the buttons on his black shirt. "You must be my eight o'clock." His voice boomed bass notes, his eyes never left the television, where a naked blonde writhed and moaned on top of a guy half-wrapped in red satin sheets.

I stared at the television, somewhat disturbed. He pressed the mute on the remote to appease me, and looked up. "Tell your fiancée she can get dressed in that little room across the lobby. The one marked 'private.' You can wash up in that little room right there. Greg'll get you a towel."

His eyes went back to the TV. The blonde was now on her hands and knees, throwing her head back soundlessly.

"My name is Ivan." I extended my hand.

His was dry, and hot, and swallowed mine. "Yeah, sure, I'm Reverend Cotton. I'll see you at eight sharp. I got a 9:45 coming in. You're lucky we could fit you in."

I left, so he could turn the volume back up.

She stole my breath as I watched her glide across the hotel lobby. She smelled like vanilla oil. "You clean up pretty good." She smiled at me, eyes sparkling. She was almost a foot taller than me in heels. "You ready?"

I nodded, and took her hand. "Wait till you get a load of Reverend Cotton."

But only Greg was in the office, looking apologetic. He was sunburned, and balding, and his jeans were too tight. "I told the Reverend you were two women, and he took off. Says he's morally opposed to that kind of thing. Sorry, girls." He shrugged and swallowed.

"You mean the guy who was watching pornos in the chapel was morally opposed to marrying us?" My voice was still calm, but my stomach was made of lead.

"Yeah, I guess so. He said he could lose his license. He said he could do it for five hundred cash, but I didn't know if you had that kind of money on you. He left me his pager number. I can call him if you want." Greg stood on one leg, then the other.

"So ... he is morally opposed, unless we have five hundred dollars." I spoke slowly, and with reason. "Greg, you understand that five hundred dollars American is like ... two million Canadian? Come on, you can get married at midnight by a man dressed as Bette Midler in this town. Are you telling me nobody will marry us?"

Greg shook his head sympathetically, and then looked pensive for a moment.

"Tell you what, I've seen a million of these things, I set up the video and work the CD player all the time, I could marry you. I mean, it wouldn't be legal whichever way, since you don't have a license, and all. I'll give you a real nice ceremony." His voice got more confident as he continued. "I got no problem marrying you, you seem like nice enough folks. I had a girlfriend once, left me for an esthetician named Alice, no hard feelings, we're still friends, whatever makes her happy, right?"

We both nodded. That settled it. He shook my hand, and kissed hers.

"Just let me go put on a clean shirt."

Greg looked heartbreakingly sincere as he stumbled through our vows. He had combed his hair, too, and put on a tie. I was crying, I always do at weddings. She was laughing like Christmas morning.

"Do you take this . . . Ivan . . . to be your lawfully wedded . . . life partner. . . ."

I loved her, and I loved Greg, and I loved this tiny chapel transformed at that moment by the three of us together into a magic place where something could be happily ever after and then . . . he stopped.

"Fuck." Both of his hands slammed onto the pulpit with a tinny echo. We looked up, startled to find carpet under our feet again. "I'm sorry, you guys, I forgot to turn the camera on. We have to do it again. Video comes with the cost of the ceremony."

My lovely almost-bride spoke first. "Okay, Greg, but can we take a smoke break before we try it again?"

Greg had his feet up on his desk, in the office, smoking a Lucky Strike. Turns out he was a roofer, from Death Valley. "Hot work, hot place, had to get out." He explained. "Tried a few things, ended up here, I like it just fine. Meet lotsa people, I get to take pictures. I'm a pretty good amateur photographer, if I do say so myself."

I believed him. He was, at that moment, my hero.

"Well, let's get this show on the road before Reverend Cotton comes back for his 9:45. You ready?"

We were, by now, most definitely ready. On our way back into the chapel, I took him aside.

"Greg, now don't get me wrong, I think you're doing a great job, but since we've got a second chance here, can I ask you a favour? Can we just drop the life partner stuff and go with the man and wife thing? I appreciate what you're trying to do for us here, but just go ahead and marry us like you would anyone else, okay, my friend?"

He nodded sincerely. Of course, if we were anyone else, he would be running the CD player, but he got my drift.

"Okay, Ivan, whatever you want, you know, I'm just trying to make it special for you both, and some of you ladies who come in from L.A. and stuff would get real . . . well, you know, offended by that kind of thing."

I put my hand on his shoulder. "Well, Greg . . . we aren't those kind of ladies."

We made it to Death Valley just before dawn. As a dusty orange sun rose over the salt flats and a honeymoon wind blew tumbleweeds under our tires, I kissed my wife and my wife kissed her bride.